The Independent Bookworm

ABOUT THE BOOK

Once upon a time in a world where magic and technology collide with unexpected consequences…

When neighboring royals visit the kingdom, Prince Laurent declines the princess' advances with dire consequences. Turned into swans, he and his brothers flee, followed by their sister in a flying machine. But then, they crash-land on a cemetery. Can they regain their humanity before the enraged princess catches up with them? And what about the strange ghost Laurent feels drawn to?

What if Hans Christian Andersen overlooked "The Seven Swans" part in breaking the curse?

ABOUT THE AUTHOR

Ever since she was born, Katharina Gerlach had her head in the clouds. She and her three younger brothers grew up in the middle of a forest in the heart of the Luneburgian Heather. After romping through the forest with imagination as her guide, the tomboy learned to read and disappeared into magical adventures, past times or eerie fairytale woods.

She never returned to Earth for long, although she managed to successfully finish training as a landscape gardener, study forestry and gain a PhD. But then, she discovered her vocation: storytelling and realized she'd have to write to make her dream of sharing her stories with others come true.

Katharina loves to write Fantasy, Science Fiction and Historical Novels for all age groups. At present, she is writing at her next project in a small house near Hildesheim, Germany, where she lives with her husband, three children and a dog.

Mehr Informationen: http://de.KatharinaGerlach.com

ROYAL SWANS

THE WILD SWANS
TREASURES RETOLD 7

Katharina Gerlach

Royal Swans, Treasures Retold 7
published by the Independent Bookworm, USA und D
This book is also available as eBook. It has been published in English and
in German.

If you find any typos or formatting problems in this eBook, please contact
the publisher (www.IndependentBookworm.de).

© 2016, all rights remain with the author
© 2016, cover art by Katharina Kolata
© 2016, title background by Corona Zschusschen
© 2014, logo by colorgraphix
© 2014, paragraph divider by Katharina Kolata
editor: Ethan James Clarke
printed On-Demand Publishing LLC, 100 Enterprise Way, Suite A200,
Scotts Valley, CA 95066, USA, www.createspace.com

ISBN-13 978-3-95681-074-9

More Information can be found on the publisher's website:
http://www.IndependentBookworm.de

For my family. I couldn't have done it without you.

TABLE OF CONTENTS

ROYAL SWANS

Blah, blah, blah, Laurent thought as he walked behind his parents and the visitors, listening to the babble of the technician who took them through the hangar and the visiting prince's questions. Little Michelle—well, at fifteen she wasn't all that little any more—always enjoyed the avian hangar, especially since several of the airship designs sprang from her mind, but he could do without looking at the giant balloons. However, it was his duty as the crown prince to show the visitors around. *I really wish Ma and Pa wouldn't take this crown prince stuff so seriously.*

The foreign princess's fingers rested lightly on his hand. Still, he would have loved to shake them and go hunting with his brothers. Only the occasional glare from his mother forced him to stay. On top of that, he seemed to be getting a headache. He felt as if an invisible hand was poking through his brain. He did his best to push the pain aside and concentrated on the airships, the kingdom's pride.

"I'd so love to see the inside of one of the gondolas," Princess Elsa said. "Would that be possible?"

"Of course, but there's only room for a handful of people." The technician smiled. "We're currently testing several designs that'd allow for more passengers per gondola."

Laurent saw his chance and lifted his hand. "I'll wait here."

When the princess, her brother, and her parents climbed aboard one of the ships with his father and the technician, his mother stayed with Laurent. He groaned.

"Stop behaving like a child, Laurent." She adjusted his collar. The small nudge at his spine made his headache worse. "You'll be twenty-four in a few more days and will have to supervise the kingdom when we travel. You need to face unpleasant duties."

"Why do you have to leave in the first place? What's so darn interesting about a fleet of steam-driven boats."

"Watch your language, son!" The queen turned to the movable stairs that had been pushed against the passenger box of the cigar-shaped airship and folded her hands in front of her chest. "Your father and I haven't had a holiday since he took the crown thirty years ago. Elsa's parents are our best friends, and this is the first time in many year that they managed to visit. Also, we'd like to see if the steam-boats might be a way to improve safety on long-distance shipping. We'll only be gone for a week or two." She looked at him over her shoulder. "But that means you'll have to bear the responsibility for that long."

He sighed again, and then they waited in silence for the others to return. Elsa was the first to hurry down the stairs. "I didn't know your brothers built half of your fleet," she said when she put her hand on his again.

"Yes, Francois and Didier are quite talented." He forced himself to smile.

"I don't know." Elsa sneered. "They must be getting awfully dirty. It's not really work for royalty, is it?"

"In a royal family with one daughter and seven sons, there's no shortage of replacement crown princes." Laurent felt his patience wearing thin. "If they enjoy working with machinery, they are allowed to do so."

"They're lucky that I'm not their mother then." Elsa flipped back a strand of her well-coiffured blond locks and batted her eyelashes at him. "By the way, do you plan on many children when you become king?"

"With the right wife, I'll take it as it comes." It was the most diplomatic answer he could muster. It took a real effort to keep from screaming, *That's none of your business, snoopy cow.* He was rewarded by a proud smile from his mother and felt better immediately.

"From me, my future husband can expect one heir, that's all." Elsa pointed to the open hangar doors and called to the royals ahead of them. "Can Laurent and I go for a walk in the park? The weather is so lovely, and this hangar rather stifling."

Laurent's gaze went through the gigantic hall with two big double doors at either end. Both of the gates were open and a warm, summery breeze floated gently through the hall, tugging at the airships' riggings. There wasn't a trace of stifling heat, so Elsa's request must be a sorry excuse for getting away from a boring afternoon. That he could understand. Maybe he could shake that headache if he walked in the sun. He felt as if the pain was lifting already, so he nodded. "I'd very much like that." The words had barely left his mouth when he wondered why he supported her.

"I don't want to leave." Elsa's brother stood with his feet apart and his hands folded behind his back. "I find the airships fascinating and would like to see more."

The grown-ups looked at each other. In the end they shrugged, and Laurent's father said, "If it pleases you, you're free to go."

Laurent loved this phrase, especially when he longed to take it literally. Smiling brightly, he left the hangar with the foreign princess at his side. He led her into the garden. There was a nice bench near the lake where he could leave her. She'd like it there and would easily find her way back to the castle since the path went straight toward it.

When she lowered herself gracefully onto the bench, she patted the seat beside her. "Sit with me, Laurent. I've decided that, since our kingdoms lie side by side, you would make a great husband. So I'd like to get to know you a little better."

"Husband?" Laurent took a step backward. "I'm not ready for marriage yet."

"But that's what this whole visit is about." Again she batted her eyelashes. "Haven't your parents told you? To unite our kingdoms, we'll get married upon their return."

For the first time since the visitors arrived, Laurent looked into her eyes. They were of a watery blue that reminded him of ice, and he shivered. The headache intensified and made it hard to think. Still, he knew exactly what he didn't want.

"I'm not going to marry anyone any time soon." He bolted. *That girl is stone crazy. There's no way I'll ever marry a girl I don't even know.* As fast as his legs would carry him, he hurried toward the stables. Maybe the peace in there would cure his pain and make him forget the princess, at least for a while.

When Laurent left the hangar, Michelle considered for a few seconds whether she should follow him. There was something strange about the foreign princess, but she couldn't put her finger on it. But then, the foreign crown prince walked to the next airship, and she turned back to him. She slipped a little forward to see him better. The gangway above the airships made the best hiding place ever.

"I like this one best," the prince announced.

The technician nodded. "You've got a good eye, sir. Michelle One is the fastest bird we've got."

Michelle tried not to look smug. True enough, Michelle One was her best work yet. She wondered what the technician would say when she showed him her new bird-of-prey design. The one person, motorized gliders would allow messengers to travel much longer distances in a much shorter time. Daydreaming about it, she nearly missed that her family and their guests were leaving the hangar.

Hurriedly, she tiptoed to the ladder that'd take her down from the raised metal boardwalk. It wasn't easy to walk the metal construction noiselessly but she'd had enough time to train, so she reached the ground shortly after the hangar had emptied. She kept close to the gate as she looked around for the visitors. They were headed to the gardens. Great. That'd be the perfect place to run into them "by accident." Michelle hurried to one of the side entrances and marched across a well-kept lawn toward the central lake. She was sure her family would be headed there since it was the most beautiful part of the garden. The path she'd chosen would take her to the lakeside, making it look to the visitors as if she'd stumbled upon them during her own wanderings.

Michelle felt her heart beating faster at the thought of getting closer to the prince. *Maybe he'll even kiss my hand. He must be grown up already.* She shivered happily. When she reached the lake, the other princess was sitting on the bench looking in the direction of the approaching royals.

"Where's Laurent?" Michelle's mother asked.

"He left, but I do believe I'm at fault." The princess cocked her head coquettishly. "I told him about the planned wedding, and he bolted."

"What wedding?" The queen's brow furrowed for a moment, then it smoothed and her smile returned. "Of course. Your wedding with my eldest son. We've got everything prepared. As soon as we're back from our travels, we'll unite our kingdoms through you."

"It will take him a while to come to terms with the idea, though," the king added. "But rest assured, he will agree to the marriage."

Michelle frowned. This didn't sound one bit like her parents. Something was really strange here. Instead of going closer, she hid in the bushes and watched, but the rest of the conversation only touched unimportant topics and travel preparations. When everybody rose to go for lunch, Michelle was none the wiser.

After feeding his stallion, Laurent pressed his face against his mane. The scent always calmed his nerves. He stood like that, enjoying the occasional nudge or snort of the animal, until it was time for lunch. Royal duties ... How he hated them. With a sigh, he left the stable and walked toward the serving room. Surely his parents wouldn't force him to marry Elsa. It wasn't like he disliked her–well, not much anyway–but they didn't even know each other. He couldn't just marry a stranger. His parents would have to see that. Maybe they would agree on some more time so he could find the good sides of his bride-to-be. The word alone sent shivers down his spine.

When he entered the room, only Michelle and Albert, his youngest brother, were there. The five-year-old ran to him and hugged his hip.

"Laurent, I want to ride," he said. His light brown hair stuck out in all directions.

"Did you wash your hands?" Laurent smiled.

"Of course!"

"But you didn't comb your hair." Laurent sat down, put the boy on his knees, and jogged him up and down.

"Thehehere wahas noho tihime." Albert giggled, but Laurent looked to Michelle, who stood motionless, watching him with a grim smile.

"What's wrong?" he asked her.

"They're going to marry you to that princess after their return." Michelle leaned against the wall and crossed her legs. In her leather pants, she looked like a boy with too-long brown

14

hair. "Something's fishy about that. It's not at all like our parents to force one of us into a marriage."

"They know about the wedding?" Laurent's eyes widened. "I thought it was all Elsa's and her parent's idea."

"Nope." Michelle walked to her place. "They're all in on it, as if they've been brainwashed."

The door opened and the royal couple and their visitors entered, followed by the usual flurry of servants. Soon, tasty appetizers, small sandwiches, and pieces of fruit were offered on silver platters and wine or juice poured into silver goblets. Everything was much more posh than their usual midday meal, but it was quieter as well, since his five brothers were still out hunting. Laurent kept silent and watched the others indulge in the delicacies. Elsa had obviously decided to follow her parents' wishes because she stayed at his side as if glued to him and talked about grain taxes, the prices of jewelry, and the difficulties of finding a good cook. He longed to throttle her, but kept his temper. It wasn't her fault that she was a spoiled, boring brat.

"Laurent," his father said after a while. "I'd like you to take Elsa out for a ride. She expressed interest in the game park."

"Naturally, Father." Laurent bowed stiffly, trying to suppress his annoyance. He shot Michelle a glance, but his sister was too preoccupied with the foreign prince. It occurred to Laurent that he didn't even know his name. Well, if he was anything like his sister, he wouldn't waste his time asking. He put aside his plate and offered his arm to Elsa. "Would you like to come now?"

"I'd be delighted." She put her hand on his again and they left the room together. Outside, she said," I'll need to get changed into something more suitable. If you don't mind, I'll meet you in the stable in ten minutes. I'll be riding side-saddle."

Glad for the break, Laurent waited for his sister and brother. She left the room with a rather idiotic expression on her face, all soft and dreamy. He laughed.

"Wow, that boy must have made quite the impression on you," he said, taking Albert's hand.

"That boy's name is Jorge." The way Michelle pronounced the name made it clear she wouldn't let Laurent walk over her feelings.

He knew that tone very well, so he didn't comment any more than simply adding, "I just hope he's less boring than his sister."

"I was wondering about that too." Michelle took Albert's free hand and together, they walked toward the stable. "But when we talked, he was … I don't know how to explain this … for me, it was perfect."

"He explained how to play frog-hop to me," Albert said. "I'll try it with my friends in the afternoon. You can have a try as well, Michelle."

She smiled down at him, and Laurent noticed there was just as much adoration in her gaze as when she had looked at Prince Jorge. The tower clock rang half past, and Laurent sighed.

"I'd better get going. Father'd be angry if I let her wait in the stables." He hugged Albert, patted Michelle's shoulder and marched off, feeling as if he was heading to his own execution.

In the stable, he chose a peaceful mare for the princess and told one of the stable boys to get her ready. Then he led his stallion outside, tied him to one of the rings in the stable wall and began to clean him. He worked slowly, thoroughly, and methodically. The well-known work relaxed his muscles and his mind. When he was done, he saddled and bridled the horse and looked around. The task had taken him the better part of half an hour, but the princess was still not there; only the mare he had chosen for her stood ready, tied to a ring close to his stallion. Laurent had just decided to find a servant to send to the princess, when Elsa swept down the castle's main stairs and walked toward one of the guards. Her fingers dug into the ear of a serving girl, who screamed with pain.

Laurent frowned and went to investigate.

"This wench has deliberately ripped my best dress." Elsa's enraged scream carried over the whole yard, and everybody stopped to look at her and the crying girl. "Put her in the dungeon for a week. No food."

"It was an acci–" The girl howled when the princess yanked at her ear.

"Liar!"

The guard looked worried. His gaze flickered from the princess to Laurent and back. Laurent nodded to him and with visible relief, he saluted and marched away.

"We do not handle things that way," Laurent said to Elsa, grabbed her hand and forced her fingers apart.

"How dare you?" The princess shot round, her face contorted with rage, but when she saw who she was talking to, her features relaxed into a smile. "Oh, Laurent, darling. Of course we'll do it your way. But the girl does need to be punished. My dress is ruined."

"There's a tiny tear in the lace," the girl said, still sobbing. "It can easily be mended. My mother is–"

"You may go." Laurent cut her off, then turned to Elsa. "We will have your dress mended in time for your departure. However, if you insist on a new dress, the treasury will cover the necessary expenses. Now, let's go for our ride before I change my mind."

There was a defiant sparkle in the princess's eyes, but her smile remained sweet as she followed him to the stable. He helped her onto her horse and mounted his stallion. In silence, they rode out of the palace's gates, through town and toward the forest. When they turned off the main road, Elsa urged her mare into gallop.

"Catch me if you can."

Rolling his eyes, Laurent nudged his horse. The stallion didn't need much persuasion. It darted off and overtook the mare in no time. Laurent glanced over his shoulder as they

17

passed. A deep frown appeared on Elsa's forehead, and she used her whip to force the mare to run faster. Laurent slowed his stallion to a light canter, then to a trot, and then he stopped. Elsa stopped too.

"What's wrong now?" Her tone was a lot less friendly than before.

Wordlessly, Laurent pointed at the bloody streaks on the mare's flanks.

"So what? It's only an animal, and she wasn't going fast enough."

Laurent didn't talk. He didn't trust himself to stay calm, so he simply ripped the rains from her hands and rode slowly back toward the town. With every minute they rode in silence, the headache he'd felt this morning returned and grew stronger. Laurent forced himself to ignore it. His boiling blood was enough to keep the pain at bay.

The minute they entered the courtyard, he stopped. Without looking at the princess, he said, "Get off."

Piercing pain shot though his head, and he closed his eyes for a second to cope with it. There was no time for a headache. He'd have to talk to his parents. Now, before Elsa came up with a story. He concentrated on what he had to say. "Go to your room and stay there until dinnertime. And never, ever dare to come near me or one of our horses again." His headache intensified with every word he spoke.

"You will regret that." Elsa's voice was low and hoarse with barely controlled anger. And it only rang through his mind. "LOOK AT ME!"

His head snapped around and his gaze locked with hers. A wave of pain rolled down his spine, as if burning iron was poured over his back. Laurent's lips moved on their own, trying to form words. With all the strength he could muster, he clamped his mouth shut. The princess's frustrated scream rang inside his head. *Get out of my mind.* Laurent tried to close his eyelids to

18

break eye contact, but his muscles wouldn't obey. He breathed in deeply, gathered his strength and kicked his stallion in the flanks. The horse reared, and Laurent's gaze was free. Relieved, he noticed that the headache was gone and his muscles obeyed him again.

"Don't you dare to do that again," Laurent said, deliberately looking at the mare and not the princess. "If you tamper with anyone's mind again, I'll denounce you as an evil witch, and you know what they do with evil witches in your kingdom."

The princess snorted but remained silent. Slowly she climbed off her horse.

"Guards!" Laurent called, and two men came running. "Take her to her room, and make sure she remains there until dinner. Under no circumstances look into her eyes."

"I swear by all that's me, you'll live to regret this." Elsa's voice was barely audible, but she used her mouth to speak this time. Laurent took that as a sign that his threat worked.

When the guards had marched her away, he took the horses back to the stable and left them in the capable hands of the stable master before he set out for his parents.

In Laurent's room, Michelle watched her brother and two of his friends snip copper coins against the wall with the help of a second coin. The one whose coins managed to hit the wall was allowed to collect all the coins and keep them. The three boys had been at the game for several hours already, and so Michelle had lain on the sofa and daydreamed about Prince Jorge, pretending to read.

A maid entered with a pitcher in her hand.

Annoyed by the disturbance, Michelle frowned. "I thought you were done here."

"Sorry, milady, I forgot to refill the drinking water." The maid curtsied. She had a faraway look on her face that made

Michelle wonder how much extra work the visitors really were. Her annoyance evaporated.

"It happens to the best of us." Smiling, she put her bookmark on the page she'd not read and closed the book.

The girl walked to the table and refilled the empty water carafe Laurent always kept close at hand. On the way to the door, she looked at the boys and said, "I'm sorry, Prince Albert, but the cook needs her sons. Could you spare them for a moment?"

Albert jumped up. "Will we get cookies?"

"I'm afraid not. She just needs to talk to them." The maid smiled. "They'll be right back."

"Oh alright..." Albert sounded instantly bored. "Can I have a glass of water then?"

"Of course." The maid filled a glass and handed it to him before she left. With grim faces, the two boys followed her. It was very evident that they didn't like being summoned by their mother. Michelle had to suppress a grin.

They had barely closed the door behind them when it slammed open again and Laurent stormed in. He was clearly upset.

"I'll kill that girl." He slammed the door behind him before he noticed Michelle. "Oh, you're here? I thought you'd be in Albert's room."

"They're still cleaning the other boys' rooms. Yours was the only one they were already done with." Michelle sat up. "What happened?"

"The princess is a witch." Laurent explained what had happened after their ride. "She must have bespelled our parents, for they still insist I marry her."

"Jorge also said that there's something terribly wrong with his sister ever since her accident."

"Accident?"

"A few weeks back, they rode out for a private picnic, and she got lost in the forest. When her horse returned without her, they searched for her and found her unconscious. She had bumped her head on a branch."

"Maybe some forest witch bespelled her and now she's a witch's puppet."

"Can I have a drink?" Albert stood beside the table and pointed to the water carafe. He wasn't allowed to touch it on his own. Since Laurent seemed to be preoccupied, Michelle went over and filled the glass for Albert.

"Unfortunately we can't just burn her at the stake. That'd upset her parents a lot." Laurent paced the room. "We'd need to find the witch who manipulates her."

"How are we going to do that?" Michelle set the carafe down and pressed the glass with water into Laurent's hand. Just holding it would force him to slow his pacing. "Maybe Jorge has an idea what we could do," she suggested. Her heart hammered madly in her chest and she didn't know if she'd have the courage to actually go and ask him to come to Laurent's room. At that moment, someone knocked on the door, and Laurent ripped it open.

Jorge stood in front of it. "I'm very sorry to disturb you, sir. However, my sister is ranting in her room, and I couldn't get a sensible word out of her. Would you be so kind as to explain the situation to me?" He looked so handsome despite the frown on his face and the hand on the hilt of his dagger. Michelle's heart melted, and she sighed.

"Your sister mistreated one of our horses badly, and I forbade her to go near the stables again. Do come in." Laurent handed the visibly relaxing Jorge his glass of water, closed the door after his guest, and went to fetch more water for himself.

The door slammed open again. *Poor, maltreated door*, Michelle thought, and stepped aside as her other brothers stormed in. The twins, Didier and Francois, were the first to reach the table. They shoved Laurent aside, who nearly spilled his water.

"I told you he'd have some," Didier said.

"I get first dibs."

"No, I. I'm thirstier than you."

"No, I'm thirstier."

They tried to stop each other from taking the carafe. While they struggled, Jerome grinned, took the carafe and filled two glasses—one for himself, the other for his brother Rene.

"There isn't enough for all of us anyway." Pierre turned and walked back to the door. "I'll fetch some more."

Jerome filled two more glasses and pressed them into Didier's and Francois's hands. "Cheers," he said and drank.

"I'm feeling so strange." Albert stumbled forward, holding his stomach. Michelle ran to him and caught him before he toppled into her arms. His whole body was shaking, and he retched, but nothing came.

Michelle stroked his forehead and called out to her other brothers. "There's poison in the water. Don't drink it!"

The room fell eerily silent. Then Jorge doubled over, followed by Laurent. They retched too, again without throwing up. Michelle stared at Albert, whose arms and legs shook like branches in a storm. At first she didn't notice that they were changing, but when the first feathers sprouted from his skin, she understood.

"The witch!" Her hands grew cold when she noticed all her brothers doubling over and retching. Albert's legs had shrunk and were now developing webs, and his neck grew longer. His face remained the same for a while longer. Then a yellow beak began to grow.

I need to do something! Michelle looked around, fighting the knot in her throat. *Should I tell father?* She remembered how Laurent had made it clear that their parents were under the witch's spell. For the moment, the best she could think of was finding a safe place to hide.

"We need to get to my airship." She lowered the twitching Albert to the ground. "You're turning into birds, and birds can fly." She opened a window. "I know you want to fight, but let's find a safe place first. Remember how the chaplain always said you can't win a war without a good strategy? Our first goal then is to find a safe hiding place."

Albert squawked. Michelle forced herself to turn around and look at her brothers. Most were still in the middle of changing—white feathers flew around the room and covered legs, wings, arms and black, webbed feet. Albert was the first one who'd transformed completely. Gray and forlorn, he hung his fluffy wings and his small head on the long neck.

Michelle's eyes widened. "You're swans!" She picked up Albert, who was clearly not yet able to fly, and hurried to the door. "Meet me at the hangar," she called over her shoulder to the others. "Hurry!"

When the pain subsided, Laurent tried to sit up. He couldn't, so he struggled until he stood. Bending and turning his incredibly long neck in unusual ways, he found that all his brothers and even the foreign prince had turned into swans.

"Wow, that was intense." Didier's words sounded like a squawk but Laurent understood him easily.

"That must have been quite a potent witch." Jerome wobbled to his feet and flapped his wings, testing their strength. "We're living in one of the most advanced kingdoms of this continent. It shouldn't be possible for a witch to create a spell this strong."

"Let's hunt her down and burn her." Francois fluttered to the top of the table. The carafe shattered, splashing him with the enchanted water.

"We don't know where she is and what else she can do," Rene said. "We should listen to Michelle."

"I second that," Jorge said. "We should hide away until we know more about this enchantment."

Everybody turned to Laurent for a decision. He was just about to say something when he heard Elsa's voice from the corridor.

"Kill those filthy birds. They're ruining the princes' rooms."

"Out!" Laurent called and flapped his wings. To his great surprise, he was airborne immediately. It took him less than a few seconds to understand how he had to move his wings. It was as if his body knew instinctively how to go where he wanted to. He shot through the window, followed by six big, white swans.

"Whoopee!" Didier soared past him high into the sky. "This is incredible!"

Laurent followed him.

Boom! A bullet whizzed past his ear.

"Higher!" He strained his wings to climb as high as possible, and the others followed.

Another bullet missed them by inches. Francois flinched and a few feathers sailed to the ground, but he still managed to keep up.

Laurent looked down at the window of his room, wondering how many guards Elsa had recruited to shoot at them. Pierre was standing in the window, taking aim again. Elsa clung to his arm and pointed. Laurent looked to the hangar, where Michelle was just running through the doors with Albert in her arms. The young swan slowed her down considerably. Laurent feared that she wouldn't be able to flee in time. After all, it took time to warm up a motor properly so it wouldn't fracture when it was used.

Boom! This time, Laurent felt the breeze of the bullet as it went past his rear.

"Higher!" he called, and everyone obeyed. He felt like a traitor leaving Michelle and Albert behind, but he couldn't help them like this. Maybe he could buy them enough time if he got Pierre to follow him in a wrong direction. "When we're in the clouds, you'll fly north," he said to Jerome. "Find a safe place and make sure Michelle can find you but no one else."

"What's your plan?" Jerome flew closer. "Aren't you coming?"

"I'll try to make the witch believe we went some other direction."

"You know the witch?"

"It's a long story, and I'll tell it to you when we meet." Laurent remained just below the cloud cover and watched his brothers and Jorge fly higher and higher. Then he turned away and started to circle, so he could watch the ground.

A low flyer, looking very different from the airships he knew, shot out of the hangar. Through its glass top, he could see Albert strapped to a seat with Michelle behind him on a second seat. The little machine had a whirring bit at the front and two wings on either side. It looked a lot like a plump bird. Laurent didn't think it would fly, but Michelle had surprised him before.

The machine rolled over the uneven yard of the palace. People sprang aside, shouting and cursing. If he'd still had his mouth, Laurent would be smiling. As it was, he squawked.

The winged machine hopped and jumped and suddenly it was airborne. Michelle pulled it into a tight curve to avoid the wall of the west wing, and then it rose higher and higher. Laurent squawked with delight again. His little sister was a wholly different magician herself–an extremely gifted mechanic. While the little mechanical bird soared toward the clouds, Laurent noticed Pierre running out of the palace and toward the hangar with Elsa in tow and the hunting gun still in his hand. He shouted orders to the crew of one of the airships and pointed toward him.

Either the witch lied to him or he's under her spell too. Laurent turned south, rising as he went. The ship Pierre was recruiting didn't stand a chance to catch up with him. The machines needed to be warmed up slowly, or Pierre risked an explosion. Glancing back down, Laurent made sure that his brother noticed which the direction he took. His ruse seemed to work. Unfortunately, Michelle and Albert in their tiny craft also followed him. Laurent cursed under his breath. He flew higher until he broke through the clouds, hoping that the newfangled airship could go this high. When Michelle broke free from the clouds too, he hovered close to her and spoke as loudly as he could.

"Turn north!" he called. "The others are headed north. I'm only trying to divert Pierre and Elsa."

Michelle shrugged, indicating that she hadn't understood a word, but Albert obviously had. His younger brother turned his long neck and pecked Michelle's hand until she turned the steering wheel. When the mechanical bird drifted in a bow, Laurent honked, and Albert stopped pecking. The moment Michelle tried to align her machine with Laurent again, Albert started his pecking again. It took Michelle three tries to realize that she was supposed to take a different direction.

"North?" she mouthed.

Laurent tried to nod, which wasn't easy with the wind howling in his ears, but Michelle understood. Her little airship turned and headed away. Relieved, Laurent dove below the clouds again.

Pierre's airship was already airborne, but still tied to a docking pole. Several crew members with binoculars pointed in his direction. Laurent marveled at how far he could see as a bird. The world seemed so much clearer. He turned westward and flew faster. When he was sure that no one from the castle could see him anymore, he flew into the clouds again and turned back. His arms—no, *wings*—hurt a little. He wondered how much pain he'd feel when he caught up with his brothers.

"You've done that very well, Albert. I am really proud of you." Michelle pointed past his head. "Look, there they are. We've nearly caught up with them. I told you we would."

Albert squawked, and it sounded content. For the longest time, they flew silently over gently rolling hills and patches of woods. They passed several villages, always trying to stay out of sight. When Laurent caught up with them, the swans began talking in honks and squawks. Michelle wished she could understand them.

"Hey, shouldn't we find a place for the night?" Michelle pointed at the sun in the west that hung over the horizon like an orange ball. Laurent honked once and took the lead. The birds began to circle in wide arcs, and Michelle did the same. With a worried frown she noticed that the wood gas she'd been using as fuel for her machine was nearly empty.

"We've got to get down soon or I'll crash the ship," she said. Albert fluttered his wings and twisted his neck toward her. She smiled soothingly. "We've still got enough for another half hour. I'm sure Laurent will find something."

Ten minutes later, they neared a small village built at the lower slope of a high hill. The top was covered in forest, and the rest of the landscape was either filled by fields or houses. Since the landscape had been much the same for the last hour or so, Michelle was sure they wouldn't find anything more suitable. And sure enough, Laurent soon began to fly lower.

When they came close, they discovered a chapel with a small lake close to the forest. A huge cemetery spread from it to the forest's edge. From above, it looked like a tree. A wide road led from the chapel nearly all the way to the forest. In regular intervals, smaller paths turned off at 90-degree angles. Like branches, they led to the sides. Again, even smaller roads split off regularly, leading toward the forest parallel to the main road. They reminded Michelle of twigs, since each led to eight gravesites. The branches with their twigs curved when they neared the outside wall, leading to more graves. The graves themselves were covered in bushes, flowers, and even trees. Although well kept, the cemetery seemed to be out of use. *The ceremonial walkway will make a great runway.* Michelle turned her airship and approached it. *I'll have no problems landing.* From the corners of her eyes, she saw her brothers and Jorge aim for the lake. *And they should be fine too.*

At that moment, the sun dropped behind the horizon. Albert screamed, and Michelle pulled the airship up instinctively. She looked around. Six human figures were hurling toward the ground. *It's so like a witch to have the curse last only for a day! I should have been expecting that.*

"Hold on tight!" she called to the seat in front of her. As fast as she could, she turned her plane and flew toward the falling young men. Luckily most of them had already been quite low over the lake, so they should get down in one piece. Only Laurent and Jorge had still been high above the others. Michelle suspected they'd been watching for danger.

Now they were tumbling toward the cemetery walls with linked hands. This gesture seemed to slow their fall somewhat. Without thinking about it, Michelle pushed her little craft into a nose dive. When she was slightly below the falling men, she leveled the airship and hoped for the best. She'd timed it right. Two thumps told her that Laurent and Jorge had hit the ship somewhere. Immediately the airship buckled and turned left. Albert screamed again. *They must be on a wing*, Michelle thought. *Turbulent Crap.*

She tried to compensate for the additional weight by following the curve the ship had already taken and slowly righting it. The wing groaned from the unusual strain. There was no time to fly the necessary circle and land on the ceremonial lane; she'd have to land *now* or risk a crash.

Michelle put all her eggs in one basket. She lowered the airship until the wheels touched grass. The airship bucked and bounced over the uneven ground. It slowed considerably but not enough. A jerk on the left told her that Laurent and Jorge must have lost their hold—or they jumped deliberately. Struggling, she managed to level the plane again. When she tried to turn left some more, the steering no longer reacted to her pulling. *Double crap.*

The outside wall of the chapel drew nearer at an alarming speed. Michelle knew she wouldn't be able to stop the airship in time. *If I survive this, I'll have to invent a brake for emergencies.* She flipped the kill-engine switch. It had been one of the first

28

improvements she'd made to any motor. In emergencies, it doused the burning chamber with water, reducing the risk of fires.

"Put your head between your knees, Albert," she called, following her own advice. Silently she prayed to any deity who was willing to listen. *Please keep my brother safe. Please!*

The crash jerked her forward and her safety belt dug painfully into her chest. Metal, wood, leather, and fabric flew through the air ... and then there was only pain, and she blacked out.

Laurent ran after the airship. His whole body hurt but nothing seemed to be broken. Only some blood ran from a cut on his upper arm. He hardly noticed he was screaming for Albert and Michelle. When the ship collided with the chapel's wall, some kind of gas escaped with a whooshing sound. Laurent stopped and held his breath but the gas didn't ignite.

Jorge stopped beside him, panting hard. "Do you think they survived?"

Wordlessly, Laurent walked closer and began to dig through the twisted pile of leather, fabrics, metal and wood. Ever faster, he threw debris aside. There ... a foot. Too small for Michelle.

"I found Albert," he called to the five dripping boys who were running over the meadow toward them. "We'll need a stretcher. He might be hurt." With extreme care, he lifted the airship's broken pieces off his youngest brother. Albert was still strapped into his seat and curled up like a baby. He was sobbing. Relief flooded through Laurent. He was sure that his brother's fetal position had saved his life since a twisted metal beam had passed just over his bent shoulder and speared the former ceiling. "Everything will be okay, Albert. Are you hurt?"

Albert didn't answer.

"I found Michelle. She's alive!" Jorge's voice came from Laurent's right, and his news were more than welcome. "But she's bleeding. We'll need bandages."

With flying fingers, Laurent unbuckled his younger brother and probed his body gently. When Albert still didn't scream from pain, he dared to pick him up. Immediately, Albert wrapped his arms around Laurent's neck and hid his face in his brother's shoulder.

"I'm never gonna fly again," he said. "Never, ever."

"Sssshhh." Laurent patted his back and carried him toward his other brothers. When he reached them, he began ordering them around. "Francois, find an easy-to-open vault or open the chapel. Rene, go through the debris and look for Michelle's emergency food box and the blankets. She always puts stuff like that into her ships, so there must be some in here too."

The two brothers turned and ran.

"Jerome, Didier, fetch whatever you can for timber and get a fire started. Use the wood from the crashed ship if necessary. Do not enter the woods; we don't know its dangers yet."

"There's a big town on the other side of the woods," Jerome said. "I saw it from higher up. We can go there in the morning and ask for help."

"The village is closer," Didier said.

"For now, it's most important to get a fire going. Michelle is hurt and we can barely see. Also, the nights are quite chilly already, so stop arguing and get going."

The brothers loped off. Laurent carried Albert to the cemetery's wall and sat him down. "Are you brave enough to stay here so I can fetch Michelle?"

When Albert nodded, Laurent turned back to the crash site. He found Jorge cradling Michelle's head, fighting back tears.

"I should have told her how much I enjoyed our chats," he whispered.

Laurent put a hand on his shoulder. "Crying won't help. Let's get her out of this."

Jorge sucked in his lower lip and gently pushed his arms under Michelle's back. She moaned. Laurent took her feet. Although his sister was big for her age, she was slender and not too heavy. Together they carried her to Albert and lay her on the ground.

Laurent tried to find out if she was badly hurt, but the light of the waxing moon wasn't enough.

"Do you think we'll stay in human shape now?"

In his worry for Michelle, Laurent had forgotten all about Jorge.

"I don't know. But don't let's worry Albert." He glanced at his brother to find him asleep. The day had been most tiring for the five-year-old.

Jorge took off his jacket and covered Albert with it. "I just thought that if I were a witch who turned people into animals, I'd make darn sure they'd never be fully at home in either world."

Laurent had to admit that Jorge had a point there. "For now, we're human. Let's make the best of it."

"Fine by me. I was just wondering." Jorge bent forward and squinted at Michelle. "How badly do you think she's hurt?"

"I haven't got the slightest idea, and I can't look if I don't have enough light." Laurent bent forward until his head nearly touched Jorge's and squinted too. There was a dark patch on Michelle's chest that could be blood or motor oil or any other fluid used in airships. "Where's Jerome and Didier got to?"

A light appeared above them and shone on the group. Laurent didn't look up.

"It took you long enough," he said. "Shine over here, so I can see better." The light drew closer and Laurent studied the damage. When he saw the huge gash in Michelle's chest and the blood-caked shirt, he cursed.

"She won't make it, right?" Jorge spoke so low that Laurent barely heard him, but he was grateful because he preferred Albert not to hear the truth just now. He nodded confirmation to Jorge, fighting the tightness of his throat.

"Don't tell the others yet," he said.

The light pushed between him and Michelle. Only now did he notice that it wasn't an ordinary light like the torch he'd expected. The ball of light hovered on its own without anyone carrying it, and it began to sink toward Michelle. What if it burned her? He needed to chase it away. Without thinking about it, he grabbed for the light. It stopped and allowed his fingers to pass through it. A tingling wandered up his arms, carrying a wave of peace to his mind. He closed his eyes. A soft voice seemed to be singing in his mind, and he longed to meet its owner. When his shoulder itched, he opened his eyes again and looked. The gash was healed. His jaw dropped.

"You want to save her?" The ball of light didn't answer but it hovered a little closer to Michelle. He waved it on. After all, they had nothing to lose. Michelle would die if the light's help wasn't enough. It dove for the chest wound and covered it.

Laurent felt like he was in a dream. A surreal light on a moonlit night beside a cemetery ... life couldn't become stranger than that, he mused. Could the light be a ghost? A person cursed to do good until some old debt was paid? Or was it a new invention he just hadn't heard of yet?

Jorge, touched his arm. "Look. It's healing." His voice sounded awed.

Laurent looked closer too. True enough, the wound was closing and had stopped bleeding. Would that be enough? He'd heard of people dying from losing too much blood, and Michelle must have lost a lot considering the condition of her clothes. Surely there was no way to replace her loss. For the first time in a very long while, he folded his hands and prayed to the god of his ancestors again.

After a while, he noticed that the light grew dimmer; then it winked out. His heart felt as if someone had cut off a piece.

"Wait!" He grabbed for it as if he could bring it back. "Don't go."

Flickering on and off, it reappeared, visibly struggling. Then it hovered up and to the top of the cemetery wall where the flickering grew less erratic. It seemed to draw strength from the graveyard.

Michelle moaned and sat up. "Whoa, my head is killing me." She grabbed it with both hands. "What happened?"

Laurent left it to Jorge to explain. He needed to know more about the light. "I'll be back in a few minutes." He hugged his sister, got up and climbed the wall. When the light flew away slowly, he followed. After a while they reached a circular fountain in the center of the cemetery. The light sank to a bench beside it. It changed form, growing longer and sprouting arms, legs and a head. It became humanoid and distinctly female, but without individual features. Laurent didn't know if it did that to make it easier on him, but he liked the form the light took. It felt familiar. He sat down beside it.

"Thank you for saving my sister. I don't know how I can ever repay you."

"Break my curse." The light didn't have a mouth to speak with. Still, he'd heard the words clearly, spoken by a soft alto voice that made him tingly all over.

"How do I do that?"

"Find the witch who cursed me and kill her." The light grew stronger again, as if this place was somehow feeding her energy.

"You seem to be no weak witch yourself," he said, trying not to sound accusing. In fact, he was extremely grateful for her abilities right now. "Why don't you kill her yourself?"

"I tried to take away her magic to stop her from harming others…" The light sounded as if lost in memories. "But she found out. Before I could finish the ritual, she cursed me to be a ghost in this cemetery. I cannot wander far from it without losing my strength, and I can talk to no one unless sitting on this bench at night. How many people do you think are visiting a supposedly haunted graveyard at night?"

Laurent didn't think there'd be many. "So your true form is that of a witch?"

"Yes." The voice grew weaker. Alarmed, Laurent looked up and noticed that the sky was already brightening again. Soon the sun would be up.

"What does the evil witch look like?"

"I'm not at liberty to tell you." Although the waif was featureless, Laurent had the feeling she smiled. "I'm not at liberty to tell you a lot of things connected to the curse. Will you still try to save me?"

"Of course I will." There was nothing else to say than that. His own spell was simply a minor nuisance. He'd find a way to use it to his advantage. For now, it was enough to sit beside the fading, human-shaped light and watch the morning sun rise.

With the first rays, the pain of the change returned, and with it the feathers of his swan shape.

Michelle carried the last of the blankets toward the tomb. It was smaller than the chapel and therefore easier to heat, but still big enough to house eight people if they stayed close to each other. With winter approaching fast, that was essential. Albert sat on a bench near their new home and nibbled at some late-blooming flowers. He looked like a gray-feathered ball of misery.

"You really should try your wings, you know," Michelle said to him. "See how much fun the others are having." She pointed to the sky where three of her siblings were flying in spirals. She knew that the others had set out to the village to swap a few things they'd need for the gold and silver coins she'd had in her purse as soon as night fell. "I bet you'd have fun too."

He shook his head.

"Remember the day you fell off your pony?" She put the blankets into the tomb, came outside again and sat beside him. "The riding teacher insisted you get back on right away. It's the same with flying."

Albert squawked.

"I know you're scared. But flying as a bird is very different from flying in a machine."

Albert fluffed his feathers and turned his head away.

With a sigh, she stroked the soft feathers on his neck. They were no longer the fluff of a baby swan but they weren't the sleek white feathers of a grown swan either. She longed to hug her little brother, knowing full well that she'd have to wait a little while longer. Stretching, she got up and pointed to a pile of wood half hidden under a bush beside the tomb. "At least I managed to cut all the wooden parts off the airship into pieces. We won't be cold tonight."

The whole day, she'd worked her way through the broken airship, setting aside pieces that could be repaired or re-used and pulling out the timber. Meanwhile, her brothers and Prince Jorge had been flying into the forest and bringing branches, some so big that two had to carry them. Michelle was happy that she'd remembered the toolbox that was standard equipment on all airships. The saw inside was rather small, but it did what it was supposed to do. She walked into the tomb but left the door open so Albert could still see her.

"You know, I thought the villagers would come to find out what happened here last night. I bet the crash was loud enough to wake them all." She knelt down and used her tinderbox to ignite a fire. "But they haven't, and I wonder why."

Albert hopped from his bench and stretched, growing back to human shape as he did. He wasn't screaming this time, so maybe the transformation to his true form didn't hurt as much as the other way round. He came inside the tomb and crouched beside the fire. "Maybe they're scared. I would be."

"No, you wouldn't." Michelle ruffled his hair. "You're such a brave boy."

"I'm scared of flying."

"You'd be foolish not to be." Michelle poked her head through the door to look for the others. "I'm scared every time I enter an airship, regardless the size. But it also elates and excites me. I'm addicted to flying, I think."

Albert cuddled into her arm. "Will you be angry if I don't fly?"

"Not one bit." She kissed his forehead. At the same time, she spotted four people coming up the path. One of them turned off to the side while the others continued toward the tomb. "There are Jorge, Didier, and Rene. Will you be alright if I head out to see where Laurent went to?"

"Sure." Albert got up and ran toward his brothers, and Michelle slipped away unnoticed.

It didn't take her long to find Laurent. He was sitting on a bench near the circular fountain at the graveyard's center and seemed to be waiting for something or someone. A light appeared at his side. Instead of walking over, Michelle hid in the bushes and watched the ghost assume human form, if not features. *Well, a ghost surely explains why the villagers stay way,* she thought. *It doesn't explain why Laurent is here though.*

"I tried to locate the woman we've been talking about but without a description that's really hard," he said to the ghost.

"I'm sorry." The ghost lowered its head. "If I tell you more the curse will become permanent."

Michelle had to strain her ears to hear her words.

"I'll keep looking, but I wish I could do more." Laurent pushed his hair back with one hand and sighed. "And it doesn't help that I'm a swan during the day."

"Oh, that spell is easy to break," the ghost said. "You'd only need a shirt made of burning nettles plucked and primed bare-handed by a princess and woven or knitted into a simple, tunic-like shirt."

Michelle barely believed her ears. There really was such an easy way to save her brothers? She held her breath to better hear what else the ghost had to say.

The luminescent figure beside Laurent continued. "Of course, there are a few more details to adhere to, but finding a princess prepared to do manual work is the crux of breaking the spell on you."

"How do you know?" Michelle could clearly make out the awe in Laurent's voice.

"I'm a witch myself, remember?" The ghost giggled.

"Of course I didn't forget. You're far too..." Laurent hesitated, then asked, "Would you be allowed to tell me how you looked like before ... the transformation? You sound rather young, judging by your voice."

"I can't remember." The ghost flickered. "But I do remember that I turned twenty-two three weeks ago."

"That makes you nearly two years younger than me. A belated happy birthday." Laurent reached for the the hand-like appendage of the light.

Michelle grinned. It was just like her brother to fall for the most impossible girl. As silently as she could, she slipped away. Her heart was dancing. There was a way to save her brothers. Now all she needed to know was what burning nettles looked like, and how to prepare them for knitting.

Early next morning, she took off the ripped gown she was still wearing and slipped into a more sensible pair of trousers and a shirt she'd found in the ruined airship. Then she told Albert to stay in the cemetery. His squawk sounded like a question.

"I'll go into the village to earn our food." Michelle stroked his smooth feathers. "We can't keep taking their food without asking even if we pay. They'd be angry, or worse, afraid."

Albert settled back down and put his head under his wing, clearly annoyed. She blew him a kiss as she walked down the cemetery's wide central path.

Ten minutes later she reached the village. It was tiny, barely more than a handful of farms. She knocked at the first house.

It wasn't very big, but clean-looking. A couple of hens ran around it, and a cat sat on a windowsill of a stable and licked its hind leg. It seemed peaceful.

"Come in." The voice sounded old.

Hesitantly, Michelle stepped through the open door into the semi-darkness of the farmhouse. She found an elderly woman stirring a pot that smelled delicious. Her mouth watered. Two small children came running from the left hand side of the house that looked like a stable and clung to the woman's apron. A third lay in a crib not too far from the fire. It slept. Michelle curtsied. "Good morning, Madam. My name is Michelle, and I'm not from here. Can you teach me know to knit?"

The woman frowned and didn't answer.

"Please, Madam. It's really important." Michelle worried that the woman didn't even know how to knit. "I can pay for the lessons, if that's what you're wondering about."

The woman's frown remained. "Are you the swans' keeper?"

Michelle wondered if she should deny it, but she preferred the truth, so she nodded.

"Keep them out of our fields." The woman shooed the children away and returned to her stirring.

"Please, Madam, I need to learn how to knit."

"I'm no Madam. Call me Ester." The woman looked her over. "How much would you pay?"

"How much would it cost?" Michelle had long learned that she could save a lot of money if she let the other party start the barter.

"Three coppers a lesson." The woman swung the pot off the fire. "And a lesson will last one hour."

There were twelve coppers to one silver, and twelve silver to one gold, meaning Michelle had enough money to pay for years and years of lessons. She hoped that she wouldn't need that long.

"Do you know what burning nettles look like?" She handed the woman a silver coin. Only then did Ester's frown disappear.

"More'n enough of those around here. I'll show you later," she said with a wide smile, and pointed to the only table in the room. "Sit down. As soon as the tubers are diced, I'll show you the basics."

Michelle found the whole process of making yarn easy. All you had to do was pick the right kind of plant, break the stems, rip the bark off by pulling the stems through a hackle—a piece of wood with many spikes that looked like a hedgehog—and then spinning the fibers into a thread. She'd learned the process in less than a week, although her thread wasn't particularly smooth yet. She'd also learned that Ester was the children's grandmother and that she had to look after them since her daughter's death in childbirth. The father did his best to provide for his family, but like most farms in the village, he had only a few fields and he couldn't afford to hire help. Michelle's money was very welcome, as was her help with the children and in the garden.

She enjoyed the menial work. It allowed her mind to wander, and she found that it often lingered on Jorge. He'd be the first one she'd release from the spell. Maybe he could talk some sense into his sister. Michelle worked harder than ever before. She liked spending time with Ester and her family, but worried about Albert who waited for her patiently every day. *I need to learn faster*, Michelle thought.

Expecting knitting to be just as easy as preparing the fibers and spinning yarn, Michelle put all her energy into the craft. But her hands were not used to the motions she was supposed to learn, so the task went very, very slowly. After two more weeks, barely more than two hand-widths of fabric dangled from her knitting needles. Still, the upper two inches were no longer knotted or too tight.

"I think you've finally got the idea, child." Ester smiled proudly at her, as if she were a wonder. Envious, Michelle looked at the four-year-old's knitting. The little girl had insisted on learning too, and gotten the hang of it much faster than Michelle.

"It's a pity you're not a princess," she said to the girl.

Ester laughed. "A fine princess she'd make, the way she snores at night."

The girl laughed.

"Hop along, honey," Ester said. "And take your brother along."

The girl put her knitting in her basket and grabbed her brother's hand. Together they ran outside to play. Instantly, Ester's face grew grave.

"This has to be our last lesson," she said.

"I thought..." Michelle couldn't finish her sentence due to the knot in her throat.

"It's not because we don't like you. Really." Ester took her hands. "It's because of your swans. There's a new law demanding that we report all swans to the king, especially if they fly in a large group rather than as a single family. You'll need to take your animals and flee."

The lump in Michelle's throat grew. Instead of words, she simply hugged Ester. When she could speak again, she whispered, "I can't leave this place. Not yet. But I'll hide my swans. Thank you so much for the warning."

"The mayor is already writing a letter to the crown." Ester clearly looked worried. "It'll take him quite a while, maybe a month or two. He's not the best writer in the world, but there's no one else in the village who could do it. Try to be gone before he sends it off."

"I will. Promise." Michelle hugged her friend again and left, feeling as if another part of her life had come to an abrupt and unwelcome end.

"Take me to your ghost."

Michelle's request took Laurent by surprise. How had she learned about his friend? He blushed. "I don't know what you're talking about."

"The one you spend half the night talking with. Don't pretend you're stupid." Michelle put her hands on her hips. "I called her everywhere in the cemetery, and most of all beside the fountain where you always meet, but she wouldn't show herself."

Laurent was flabbergasted. He'd thought his little secret well kept.

"Laurent, this is important," she insisted. "I wouldn't ask if it weren't. Help me now before the others return."

So, sending his brothers and Jorge to fetch the usable parts of the airship had been a diversion.

"Fine." He turned and walked to the fountain in the cemetery's center. "Wait beside the fountain," he said and sat down on the bench. Immediately, the now familiar body of light formed beside him. He greeted his friend and told her that he still hadn't made much progress on finding the witch. He also told her about his father's order to report swans, which made it more difficult for him to search. After he shared his news, he pointed to his waiting sister and said, "Michelle would like to talk to you, if you don't mind."

Michelle stepped forward.

The person of light flickered a little but stabilized again. "What can I do for you?"

"I'd like to know more about the way to redeem my brother." She smiled. "I overheard you a while back when you told him it was easy. Let me tell you, learning to knit is anything but easy."

The figure laughed, a tinkling sound Laurent had never heard before but which sent shivers of pleasure through his body. How he longed to embrace the cursed girl. He loved her, witch or not.

"There are a couple of conditions you need to fulfill." The ghostly figure shivered. "For one, you may not talk from the minute you start working to the time the spell is broken. Neither may you shed a single tear."

"I can do that."

"You'll have to pick the nettles with your bare hands, break the stems with your naked feet, and add a drop of your blood to the shirt you knit."

Laurent felt the blood drain from his face. "You're not going to do that, Michelle. I forbid it."

"It's the only way to break the spell, and I'll do it whether you like it or not." She folded her arms in front of her chest and turned to the cursed girl again. "Do I have to knit the shirt with my own hands too or can I build a machine to do it for me?"

The girl stayed silent, maybe pondering the question. After a while, she asked, "You will build the machine without anyone's help?"

"Yes. I'll be using the parts from my crashed airship."

"Will it be powered by a steam engine?"

"No. The engine is blown. I planned on a crank-like mechanism."

"That will work. Magic is nearly incompatible with steam engine technology but not with normal mechanics." The girl nodded. "Just make sure you touch the surface of every single bit you put into the machine, and add a few drops of blood every now and then. That should bind your essence to the gadget well enough so the magic will follow the thread into the shirt."

"I don't like it. You really shouldn't do that. It'll hurt terribly." Laurent remembered the time he'd fallen into a patch of burning nettles as a child and how long the pain had lingered. He got up and put a hand on his sister's shoulder. "You can't pick nettles with your bare hands without crying. Believe me. Please. Let me look for a better way."

"There is no better way." The cursed girl got up too, keeping one foot on the bench. Her touch was light as a feather on his arm. "Even the witch's death wouldn't break this spell. It already took permanent root in your soul."

"All the more reason to do it." Michelle nodded to the ghost. "Thank you. I have to be going."

Laurent watched her walk away at a brisk pace. His heart longed to protect her, but he knew she wouldn't let him. When had his little sister become so grown up?

"She'll be fine." The girl's hand slipped into his. "And as a human, you might find it easier to break my curse too."

He turned, closed his eyes to stop them from watering, and faced the light that was her head. "I'd do anything for you, but she's my sister. I can't watch her hurt herself like that."

"You'll have to." The girl's voice was barely more than a whisper. When he opened his mouth to answer, she put a finger of light to his lips. "Ssshh. I'd like to relish the moment."

Suddenly his heart hammered like a steam engine. Ever so carefully, he bent forward and touched the place with his mouth where her lips should have been. Warmth spread through his body in a wave of longing and pleasure. A little sigh escaped the girl before she vanished from his arms. He felt her tingling touch for the rest of the night, but no matter how often he returned to the bench, she wouldn't show up again.

A few nights later, Laurent discovered that Albert had gone. He'd noticed that the little boy had been unhappy and restless for a while already since he couldn't help much with the parts Michelle needed for her machine. That's why Laurent had ordered one of the other boys to play with him, but maybe Albert missed talking to Michelle during the day and had decided to find a replacement. Laurent sent everyone in a different direction while he searched the whole cemetery. Only Michelle kept working doggedly on her machine.

"He's not in the chapel or anywhere around it," the twins announced when everyone returned close to daybreak.

"And he's not in the upper meadow," Jerome said.

"We couldn't find a trace of him in the direction of the village either." Rene looked at Jorge. "We even talked to a tramp."

Laurent opened his mouth to scold him—he'd told his brothers often enough that they needed to keep their whereabouts a secret—when Jorge interrupted.

"It was important, Laurent. The tramp had swan heads swinging from his belt and wanted to know if we'd seen any."

Laurent's throat went dry.

"From what he told us, Elsa and Pierre are hunting down every swan they can find." Jorge's voice held as much worry as Laurent's heart.

"We must find Albert," he whispered, not trusting his voice. He didn't dare voice the fear he saw mirrored in his brothers' eyes when they had heard about the swans' heads.

"Maybe we should search the forest," Jorge suggested. "It's the only place nearby we haven't looked yet."

Wordlessly, Laurent ran. It was a race against time. He had to find Albert and bring him back before the sun rose. He felt his brothers behind him, but with his long legs, he was the fastest. He reached the forest first, and true enough, someone small had broken through the undergrowth not too long ago. He sighed with relief.

"Wait here," he said to his brothers and followed the trail.

"Albert!" He formed a funnel with his hands. "You need to come back."

"Aww. But I like it here." Albert's voice sounded so close but Laurent still couldn't see him.

"The sun is going to be up any minute." He tried to keep the panic out of his voice. How was he supposed to get his little brother back to safety in his swan form? He looked over his shoulder. The sky already showed a sliver of light. He had maybe five to ten minutes left. "Please, Albert. We need to hurry."

"Alright. I'm coming." His brother stepped out of a bush and waved at it. "I'll be back tomorrow. Promise."

Laurent took his hand and they ran back, but twigs and roots snagged at them as if they didn't want to let his brother go. When they stumbled out of the undergrowth, the sky was already turning pink and red. Laurent picked Albert up and ran faster, with his other brothers on his heels. Halfway back he felt the change coming on. *No! That's still too far. Albert won't be able to walk that far on a swan's legs.* He tried to run even faster, but his legs buckled and shrunk.

When the pain subsided, he turned to Albert and wondered how they'd get him to fly. He knew that his little brother remained steadfast in his refusal to rise, and Michelle was nowhere in sight. He'd have to fetch her somehow. A blanket landed beside him on the ground, and Jorge followed.

"Michelle's busy with her machine," he said. "I thought we might be able to carry him if all of us help."

It was worth a try. They had to be back in the cemetery before any of the villagers or the tramp saw them fly. He urged the protesting Albert onto the blanket. The boy only obeyed when he told him about the headhunter tramp. When he noticed how pale Albert seemed despite his swan features, Laurent felt sick to the heart. He shouldn't have told him that. Albert loved animals.

Feeling guilty, he grabbed his corner of the blanket. When he was sure that everyone was ready, he batted his wings. They took off together. Albert huddled into a ball with his head under his wing, while his brothers strained their muscles. Luckily they didn't have to fly far. They reached the cemetery in a few minutes.

Michelle hugged them one by one, not even hesitating at Jorge. She ushered them into the tomb that served as their hideout and put a finger to her lips. Then she pointed to the village and pantomimed people walking. Laurent understood and nodded. Michelle grabbed a self-made broom and began to sweep the paths they had taken, collecting white feathers as she went.

Laurent pulled the door close as best he could and turned to his brothers whispering. "Someone is coming. We've got to be really, really quiet."

"Oh dear, that's going to be boring," Didier said.

"I'll sleep then." His twin brother Francois opened his wing and allowed Albert to slip underneath. Soon they were breathing evenly. The others followed their example. Only Jorge kept silent vigil with Laurent, staring through the crack of the door, wondering what went on outside.

When Michelle was sure that she hadn't missed a single feather in the whole churchyard, she took off the gloves she'd begun wearing during the night and returned to collecting nettles. She already had quite a stash behind their tomb, and her hands were covered in blisters. She bit her lower lip and braced herself for the pain. Under no circumstances would she weep. When the man she'd warned her brothers about arrived, her arm was full with the plants.

"Oh. I didn't know there was someone here." The man bowed, and the swans' heads swung. "Please excuse my intrusion, fair child, but have you seen some swans lately?"

Painfully aware of her none-too-clean clothes, Michelle's gaze wandered to the grisly sight at his belt and she shook her head.

"Are you sure?" He came closer.

She stepped back, holding the nettles in front of her like a shield.

"Why don't you answer? Cat got your tongue?" With two long strides, he reached her and grabbed her. Before he could pull her close, she shoved the burning nettles into his face.

Screaming madly, he let her go. She dropped the nettles and ran. As fast as her legs would carry her, she ran toward the village. Soon she heard the man following her. His footsteps came closer the longer they ran. Her heart hammered and her blood roared in her ears, but she reached Ester's farm before he could catch her. Ester's son was just coming through the door. His eyes widened when he saw the stranger running only an arm's length behind Michelle with murder in his eyes.

"Stop right there, or I'll run you through." He lowered his fork. Panting hard, and extremely grateful for her good luck, Michelle hid behind him.

The stranger stopped. "You will regret that. I swear." He turned and walked back to the cemetery. Michelle worried that he might find her brothers, but right now there was nothing she could do.

The farmer turned to her. "Girl, ye're trembling. Get yerself inside. I'm sure Ester still has some porridge left, and the childers will be happy to see you again too."

Michelle nodded and went indoors. When Ester welcomed her with open arms, she very slowly began to relax. Naturally, Ester bombarded her with questions, but Michelle didn't answer. She only shook her head and pointed to her throat.

"Oh, you can't speak because of a cold. Poor child." Ester took her hands and then stared at them in shock. "Dear me, what a rash. What did you do?"

Michelle shrugged.

"Wait, I've got just the thing for it." Ester hurried into her bedroom and returned with a pot of white salve which she spread generously on Michelle's arms. "Marigold and goose-fat is good for all sorts of burns, cuts, and rashes."

Michelle felt the relief immediately and sighed. She bent forward and kissed the old woman's cheek. When she returned to the cemetery at dusk with the rest of the salve, the stranger was nowhere in sight. She decided not to tell her brothers about him.

A week later, Michelle plucked the first shirt off her machine. The knitting was quite loose because she hadn't managed to reduce the thickness of the wires she used as hooks. She carried it outside and held it up to the sun. It would do.

One of the swans waddled toward her. Over the last few days, the boys had abstained from flying just in case the tramp was still around, but they obviously didn't like walking all that much since they spent most of their days sitting in the tomb's shade or swimming in the lake beside the chapel. The swan hung his head.

Michelle cocked her head questioningly and crouched. The swan lifted a wing. One of the feathers had broken and was now sticking up at an odd angle. Humming to soothe the agitated bird, she removed the feather with a swift motion. Then she threw the shirt over the swan, held her breath and waited for the magic to work. *Please, let it be Jorge,* she thought because it wasn't easy to identify the swans. *Surely he'll finally look at me if I free him first.*

The swan struggled and twisted to get out of the shirt. He squawked, clearly annoyed. When nothing happened, Michelle took the shirt off again. Her lip trembled and she had to bite the inside of her cheek not to cry. The swan hissed, turned, and ran.

Michelle fought back tears. She didn't dare to cry, before her brothers and Jorge were redeemed. What was the mistake? Did she have to put the shirt on at a special time? Maybe at midday or during the sunset? She needed to talk to that ghost, but couldn't. Dejected, she sank to the ground beside their tomb's entrance and put her head on her arms. Exhaustion overtook her and she fell asleep. When she woke, Albert was nibbling at her shirt. He'd already eaten half of it.

She glared at him and ripped it away, but when she saw the damage, she handed it back. It wasn't serviceable any more. With a sigh, she got up and went to collect more nettles. After all, she still hadn't broken the spell.

When the sun set, she put down her nettles, salved her hands and grabbed Laurent. She pointed in the direction of the fountain. He nodded. Together they walked to the cemetery's central point.

"Where are you going?" Albert jumped at them from the bushes. "Can I come?"

Michelle wanted to send him away but Laurent had already picked him up. "Of course you can come. You can meet a friend of mine, but you may not be scared."

"Why? Is he scary?" Albert looked around, wide-eyed. "Is it a ghost? There are ghosts on cemeteries. The hedgehog said so."

"So, you're talking to hedgehogs when we're not around?"

"And foxes, moles, birds, crickets. Once I even spoke to a red deer but I'd have to go to the forest again to see it." Albert pointed ahead. "Can I go first?"

"Sure." Laurent set him down and watched him bounce ahead. He grinned and didn't seem to take Albert's babbling seriously, but Michelle had often seen her little brother squawk at other animals during the day. Maybe he really was talking to them. It didn't mean they were answering though.

When they reached the fountain, the ghost was already waiting for them. Albert stood in front of it with a wide open mouth.

"Better close it or the night bugs will fly in," Laurent advised and stepped up to his friend. "Thank you for coming."

"I saw your sister try the first shirt this morning." The woman of light turned to Michelle. "I'm sorry for the failure. It was my fault. I wasn't aware that there are several cursed swans."

Michelle held up seven fingers.

"Yes, I noticed during the last few days, but I couldn't get you to see me." The light glowed darker, as if blushing. "I'm quite glad you decided to come."

Michelle cocked her head and pulled up her eyebrows in an exaggerated gesture of questioning. The ghost understood immediately.

"You want to know what you'll need to do?"

She nodded.

"You'll need to create one shirt for every swan and put them on in the order they were cursed."

Pigeon dung, Michelle thought. *I can barely remember what happened. How am I supposed to know who was cursed when? All I know is that Albert was first.*

Laurent said, "I think the first one to turn into a swan was Jorge."

Michelle shook her head and pointed to Albert.

"Oh, yes, you're right. Jorge was second. After that all is blurry." He scratched his head. "We'll have to discuss this with the boys."

Michelle nodded and had already turned to walk away when Albert grabbed her hand.

"I know the order." He looked up to her. "Because I was already a swan when all the others turned. I remember. Really."

She stoked his hair and looked at him, willing him to speak.

"When you took me in your arms, Jorge fell. And then Laurent fell. I looked to Francois, but he and Didier had just put the glasses aside. Then Rene fell, and then Jerome. The twins were last. They always do the same things at the same time. I remember that I thought it very funny."

Michelle kissed his cheek and nodded. She was proud of her little brother. Now she could get started on breaking the curse in earnest.

Laurent stayed with the ghost for a little while longer but then decided it was time to filch something to eat again. His brothers were most likely trying to hunt again, but at night that wasn't easy. He dug though his pockets for his coins, and set out for the village.

What are we going to do when the money runs out? He only had three gold pieces and a few silver left, and his brothers always had less money than he did. He was lucky he'd been carrying that much in his pocket when the curse took.

When he neared the village, he pushed the worry aside. Like a shadow, he slipped from house to house. Ever since they'd paid for the first lot of food they stole, some of the villagers sometimes left a basket with food outside. He found two and left one silver piece each. Now he was down to three gold pieces and two silver. With a sigh, he was turning to go home when he heard voices coming from the inn.

"Ann I tellya." The voice slurred the words, but Laurent could make them out nonetheless. "I gota ledder fromde cassssstle. The crown prinsh will come here endof nesht week."

"You're dreaming, mayor." The youth supporting the portly, drunk man obviously had had better sense than to drink away half the night. "Although Father would be delighted to house guests like that."

"Ann I tellya." The mayor swayed and leaned heavily on the young man's arm. "They're gonna killm dem birds–swans– whatever. And then … vanishing food and money bye, bye."

He giggled. A wave of alcohol-breath washed over Laurent as the pair passed his hiding place. He held a hand over his nose. As soon as the two were out of sight–he could still hear them argue–he picked up the baskets and hurried back to the cemetery.

"We need to leave," he said to Jorge, who sat on the wall near the entrance and was cutting a flute. Albert stood below him, waiting impatiently for his new toy. Laurent took his shoulders. "Go, fetch the others, Albert. This is really urgent."

Pouting, Albert ran off, calling for his brothers while Jorge followed Laurent to the tomb where Michelle was busy smashing nettles.

Laurent waited impatiently for his brothers to arrive. When everyone was there, he didn't bother with niceties. "We need to pack everything up and leave right away. Pierre and Elsa have found out where we are. They announced their arrival to the mayor for the end of next week."

"We can't leave." Jorge pointed to the bulky machine made from scrap metal. "Michelle's knitter is way too heavy, and without it she'll be hard-pressed to break our curse."

"And if they found us once, they'll find us again," Jerome said.

"We'd better prepare for battle," Didier and Francois said together.

"They won't fight us." Laurent didn't understand why they didn't get the situation. "They'll wait until the sun rises and then have their hunters shoot us. Our only chance to save ourselves is to find a place to hide. Maybe somewhere in the forest."

All of a sudden, he realized that leaving the cemetery also meant not seeing the woman of light again. He swallowed and forced himself not to think about it. The safety of his family came first.

"I can find us a place in the forest," Albert said. "I've got a lot of friends there."

Laurent ignored him. "Come on, boys. Let's pack."

"Just because we hide, it won't stop them from hunting us," Jorge said. "And Michelle's knitter will make them realize that she knows how to break the curse. If necessary, they'll burn down the whole forest."

"But that would kill my friends too." Albert stared at him, wide-eyed.

Jorge smiled at him. "I fear Elsa isn't interested in your friends. I don't know what got into her, but she's determined to get her revenge on us no matter what."

Michelle tugged at Laurent's arm, pointed to the sky and drew six half circles with her hand. Then she pointed to the machine and their belongings and made packing motions.

Laurent considered her pantomime for a while before he understood. "You think we should wait for six more days before we pack?"

She nodded.

"That's cutting it awfully close." Laurent felt torn. One the one hand, he'd love to spend more time with the light lady, on the other he knew that Elsa wouldn't give them half a chance. "What if they are coming early?"

"I'll be the lookout." Jorge took a step forward, grabbed Michelle's hand, and looked into her eyes. "Try to get as many shirts done as you can in the time we have. I trust you."

She blushed and nodded. They stood like that for a short moment, then she freed her hands and returned to hackle last night's nettles.

Laurent sighed and turned to the others. "Let's at least prepare for a hasty departure. We can pack everything we don't need right now and move it to a safe place in the forest. If we keep nothing but the bare necessities and pick up stray feathers every night, we can leave at a moment's notice if necessary."

The next hour was extremely busy. Everybody ran around packing whatever they thought important. Sometimes Laurent had to arbitrate, but most of the time everything went smoothly. When they took their belongings to the forest, Albert surprised everybody by finding the perfect hiding place—the hollow trunk of a gigantic oak tree.

Laurent ruffled his hair and let him choose from the baskets of food first when they returned to the cemetery shortly before the sun rose.

For the next few days, Michelle worked like mad. She barely slept, and her hands and feet grew redder and number with every passing hour. She did her best to ignore the pain. The few hours she did sleep, she dreamed of someone poking pins into her limbs and arrows into her swans.

A few hours before sunrise on the sixth day, she finally had enough yarn for seven shirts. She threaded the first ball into her knitter. Then she took a knife and sliced into the skin on the back of her hand. Blood welled up and dropped onto the hooks.

"What are you doing?" Jorge stepped beside her and ripped the knife from her hand.

She pointed to the machine, then to the ball of yarn, willing him to understand that this little sacrifice was necessary. He looked into her eyes without saying a word. Then he bent forward and kissed her lips very gently. Her heart raced and heat rolled through her. When he straightened again, she sighed longingly. It was wonderful to finally know his feelings. Before she could do anything, he sliced through the skin on the back of his hand too and added his blood to Michelle's on the machine. She opened her mouth to protest, but he put a finger to her lips. "It's obligatory."

"Hey, we want too." Didier and Francois came running with Jerome, Rene, and Albert in tow.

Jorge complied and cut them too. More red drops colored the hooks. Michelle couldn't tell them that their blood wasn't necessary, so she didn't try.

"Me too." Albert held out his small hand. Michelle shook her head, but Jorge didn't hesitate. It broke her heart to see her brother flinch when Jorge cut him, but somehow it seemed right to add everyone's blood to the task at hand. It was a symbolic gesture of support she appreciated very much.

"Laurent is still missing," Rene said. Immediately all the boys ran off to fetch him. When he saw the combined blood on the hooks, he offered his hand willingly.

"I very much hope this will work." He stared at the hooks that began moving when Michelle began to turn the crank. "We've only got one more day before they come."

"I'll be on the lookout." Jorge handed him the knife and ran off.

Michelle's heart went with him. *It'll only take two or three hours to complete all the shirts.* She attached the other balls of yarn to the automatic feeds, so the machine could run on its own if necessary, and covered the contraption with scrap metal with her free hand. She made sure that the noises the machine made weren't amplified by the covering, and then she sat beside it and kept turning the crank. She'd invented a wind-up mechanism that allowed her to let go of the crank after five minutes of turning. The machine would then run up to one and a half hour on its own.

Jorge came running. "They're coming!"

Michelle's heart dropped like a stone. She couldn't leave the machine. Not now. She was so close to breaking the curse!

When her brothers stormed into the tomb, she hid in the bushes behind her machine.

Laurent didn't need to say anything. The last few belongings were packed in no time and everyone ran off through a back gate toward the forest. Only when they reached the underbrush did he notice that Michelle was missing.

He cursed. "We've got to go back."

"We can't. Look." Jorge pointed to the cemetery, which was surrounded by soldiers.

Laurent cursed some more.

"Shall I call my friends?" Albert pushed a hand into Laurent's.

He looked down and smiled. "I'm afraid they won't be much help. We'll need to think of something else."

"Why don't we go back and talk to Pierre?" Rene asked. Laurent stared at his normally quiet brother. Rene blushed and continued. "He's hunting swans, right? If we don't dawdle too much, we could have them gone before the sun rises."

"We can't all go; it's too dangerous," Laurent said. "As the eldest, it falls on me."

"And I'll be coming along since Elsa is my sister." Jorge stood beside him, looking grim.

Laurent knew he wouldn't be able to sway him. He cut through his brothers' protests with a gesture. "Jorge and I will try Rene's idea. The rest of you stay behind to protect Albert. And be as quiet as you can."

Reluctantly, his brothers followed a deer trail deeper into the forest. Laurent nodded to Jorge, and they walked back. Since the distance between the cemetery and the forest was covered by grass, they couldn't hide and were discovered soon. Several soldiers lowered their guns, but raised them the moment they recognized Laurent.

"Sir!" A soldier saluted and others followed suit. Laurent nodded at them. Unhindered the two young men entered the cemetery and walked toward the tomb.

"I'll get Michelle out and you can talk to Pierre," Jorge whispered.

"There's no use talking to Pierre as long as he's under Elsa's spell," Laurent whispered back. "I only came to fetch Michelle."

A shadow appeared in front of them, so they ducked between the bushes. Laurent held his breath. It was the tramp they'd seen earlier. With a handgun at the ready, he slipped along the path, ready to shoot.

All of a sudden, Laurent was completely certain that he was the only one who'd shoot swans without hesitation. The soldiers would do so too, but only if they were ordered, and they'd take their time aiming. Instinctively, he grabbed the tramp's gun hand and yanked. The man stumbled forward with a small yell. Laurent took a stone and smashed it against his head. The tramp slumped. An examination revealed that he was still alive.

Jorge bound his arms and legs while Laurent gagged him. After hiding him well under the bushes of a sunken grave, they walked on. The closer they got to the cemetery's entrance, the more people milled around. It became harder to evade them but they managed to reach the tomb unhindered. Worried, Laurent looked at the sky. It was already growing lighter. They'd wasted precious time in coming here, but leaving Michelle behind was out of the question.

He marveled at her guts and her genius. The machine's crank was only an arm's length away from the tomb's door but didn't look like anything but scrap metal. Not one of the people searching the cemetery gave it a second glance. Then, he discovered Michelle's eye peeking out of the tomb.

"Find that witch." Elsa's voice had an edge to it that made Laurent's hairs stand up. "She must be here somewhere."

"And get her to me alive. I need to know if I can really save my brothers by shooting swans." Pierre's voice had changed. He sounded self-assured and competent. If the situation had been different, Laurent would have been proud of him.

He had barely registered the thought when the muzzle of a gun hit him between the shoulder blades.

"Get up very slowly." The soldier behind him sounded quite young. "If you move too fast, I'll shoot you."

Laurent lifted his hands to show he was unarmed and rose. "I'm Prince Laurent," he said and turned. "I came to talk to my brother."

"Anyone can say that." The soldier wore the uniform of Jorge's and Elsa's country.

Laurent expected Jorge to speak up for him, but his friend wasn't at his side. When he looked around, he couldn't see him either. He smiled at the soldier. There was but one thing left to do to give Jorge the chance to save Michelle.

"Take me to Prince Pierre and you'll see."

"Move." The soldier pointed in the direction he wanted Laurent to go. With his hands still raised, he walked toward the cemetery's ceremonial road. Pierre and Elsa stood beside the central well. Pierre wore his dark blue state uniform, golden epaulettes, rapier and all. A big airship was tied to the bench where Laurent's light lady usually showed up. He regretted that he hadn't been able to help her. He bit his lip. Crying over spilt milk was useless. If Pierre would let him go before he turned into a swan, he'd be more diligent in his quest for the evil witch.

"Laurent!" Pierre ran to him and embraced him. "I missed you so much. Where are the others? Where's Michelle? What happened? Elsa said you were stolen by cursed swans."

Laurent hugged his brother back. Maybe he could use the twisted tale Else had wrought against her. "That's not true," he said. "We were cursed and turned into swans."

"Incredible!" Elsa's voice cut through his soul like a knife. "Who'd do a thing like that?"

"Oh dear. My hunt for the cursed swans could have killed you. If only I had known." Pierre turned to the soldier. "Tell everyone that they're forbidden to hurt another swan. Hurry."

The soldier turned and ran off.

"Now, tell me, where are the others?" Pierre hooked his arm into Laurent's and pulled him to the bench where the ship was moored. "I want to hear all about your adventures."

"Sir?" A captain stopped in front of Pierre and saluted. "We found a girl hiding in a tomb. We've locked her in for now. What are we to do with her?"

No, not Michelle ... Laurent's heart contracted painfully. Where was Jorge?

"I'm coming." Pierre dragged Laurent along, whose heart grew heavier by the minute. Elsa followed them. When they reached the tomb, two soldiers opened the wrought iron gate, and two more dragged Michelle out. She looked rather bulky with the tatters she had knotted around her middle. Laurent needed a moment to realize that the bulge were the shirts she was producing.

"Who are you?" Pierre demanded.

Laurent's jaw fell. How could Pierre not recognize his own sister? "It's Michelle," he wanted to say but found that not a single syllable left his mouth.

"I bet it's the witch," Elsa said. "If she cursed the princes, it makes sense to stay close to them. After all, we don't know what she wanted them for."

"You're right, dear." Pierre smiled at her, and she smiled back with a decidedly wolfish grin.

Laurent wanted to protest, to shake sense back into his brother, but his body wouldn't obey. Oh, how he longed to strangle the witch! He glared at Elsa, and she smiled at him sweetly.

"Maybe the curse will be broken if we kill the witch," she said to Pierre. She was obviously enjoying herself. Laurent turned to Michelle, willing her to say something, but she stared silently at a point behind him.

A soldier screamed. Then another one. More screams followed. Soon soldiers poured past them like a tide.

"Ghosts!" The captain grabbed Pierre's arm. "We've got to take you to safety, sir."

"We're not going anywhere before I save my brothers," Pierre said. He pointed to a crossroad near the tomb. "Get some soldiers to build a pyre there. We'll burn the witch at the stake."

"Wouldn't it be much faster if you had her beheaded?" Elsa's voice sounded like the purr of a cat.

"Everyone knows that you can't kill a witch unless you burn her." Pierre turned to his captain again. "The ghosts are probably only illusions made by the witch to scare you. We won't fall for that. Collect wood now."

Laurent could see that the captain didn't like to do as he was told. The man's gaze flew from Pierre to Michelle and back, and his mouth trembled slightly as if he wanted to say something and couldn't. It was obvious that he had recognized Michelle too. Still, he saluted, turned, and called to his men as requested. Laurent wondered how many people Elsa could control with her magic. Maybe it was only one at a time.

"The girl is not the witch, Pierre." Laurent grinned when he realized that he was free to speak again. "It's El–"

A shot rang through the night and fiery pain pulsed through Laurent's shoulder. Unbelieving, he lifted his gaze from the blood on his shirt to the captain, who still stood there, wide-eyed, with the smoking gun in his hand. The world began to shrink around Laurent. Soldiers grabbed the captain and disarmed him. They pushed Michelle back into her tomb and locked the door. Laurent barely noticed hands ripping his shirt open. His gaze was glued to the sky's orange glow that mirrored the fire in his shoulder. Then the world went black.

Michelle bit back tears. She must not cry. *Not Laurent. Please!* She didn't dare to pray loudly. Now it was more urgent than ever to get the shirts done. She felt for the four she already had knotted around her hips.

"He's still alive. Fetch the physician." Pierre's voice rang loud and clear over the cemetery.

Michelle sighed with relief, sank down at the tomb's wall, and wondered about the situation. Why hadn't Pierre recognized her? Would he really burn her at the stake? If so, how long would it take him to have his men fetch enough wood? She gazed at the crank. It would need turning again soon. While she crept closer to the door, she looked for the soldiers guarding her. They had their backs turned on her, and Pierre was busy ordering people around who carried small amounts of timber past him.

"Send some men to the forest," he said. When she discovered Elsa resting on a leisure chair that someone had set up for her facing away from the tomb, she dared to push her hand through the bars. She'd calculated the distance correctly when she'd set up the machine. Very gently, she grabbed the crank, and at that moment a golden light appeared beside her. It flickered, which Michelle took as a question.

She pointed to Laurent, who had been laid in the soft grass in the shade of a tree not far from Pierre. Someone had wrapped his shoulder with cloth, but it was already bleeding through.

At the sight, the light winked out, but reappeared soon after. Michelle pointed to Elsa and made warning notions. The light bobbed up and down. She just hoped that it had understood her correctly. Non-verbal communication was extremely difficult, especially if one of the people involved was a ball of light. Michelle watched her go. The light drifted very close to the ground and hid under bushes whenever possible. Michelle grabbed the crank again. When the light settled on Laurent's chest, she was already turning the handle slowly, steadily, and nearly soundlessly, glad that she'd greased the crank's shaft well enough.

Suddenly, Elsa sprang up and pointed to Laurent, screaming madly. "The witch is killing him!"

The light winked out instantly, and Michelle let go of the crank. Before she could pull back her hand completely, the guards shot round. One of them slammed the butt of his gun on her forearm.

She howled in pain when her bones splintered. But she closed her eyes and managed with utmost concentration to keep the tears down. It was the hardest thing she'd ever done. At the same moment, the first rays of the sun blinked over the horizon, and Laurent changed. Pierre screamed too when he saw his brother's limbs twitch and morphed. The whole process only took a few seconds.

Meanwhile Michelle kept fighting the tears. The pain in her arm made her eyes water, but she managed not to cry as she cradled her arm. *Hopefully the machine has been wound well enough.* She tried to think of Jorge to suppress the pain, but found it really hard to concentrate. Loud honking told her that Laurent had changed. With delight, she watched him flapping his wings and finally lifting off. A few minutes later, he was joined by five more swans.

"Don't shoot! They're my brothers," Pierre ordered, even though none of the soldiers had made a move. "Albert, Francois, Rene, Didier, Jerome. Come down. We'll find a way to save you." But the swans didn't listen to him. They soared higher and higher until they were barely more than white specs in the sky. Pierre cursed.

"What's wrong, my dear?" Elsa stood up and walked to him to rest her hand on his arm.

"As long as they're that high up, we can't burn the witch. They'd all fall to their deaths."

Michelle drew in a sigh of relief. *Stay away,* she thought. *Please stay in the air for as long as you can.* A low swishing sound drew her gaze to the machine. Another shirt had landed not far from the crank in the grass. She looked at the soldiers, but they were staring up into the sky, where the white specs were still circling.

"Get the airship ready," Pierre ordered. "We'll catch them with nets and when they're safely on the ground, we'll burn the witch."

Immediately people began to run to and fro. Michelle was glad about that, since she seemed to be forgotten for the moment. As silently as she could, she reached out with her unhurt arm, grabbed the shirt and pulled it inside. *Just two more to go.* It was a little difficult to tie it around her waist like the others because she could only use one arm, but she managed. Then she closed her eyes and waited.

Laurent watched the airship lift off.

"They'll try to catch us with nets," he called to the others. "Are you sure Albert is up to it? He's so small." He didn't like to be dependent on a five-year-old.

"You should have seen his army," Jerome honked. "It's impressive. Now, let's buy Michelle some time."

They spread out, evading the approaching ship with no trouble. The huge, cigar-shaped balloon wasn't made for fast maneuvers, so the swans found it easy to evade it and the nets the crews tried to throw over them.

"They're coming," Jorge called. "Diversion go!"

Didier and Francois yelled with delight and dove first. Just before they reached the ground, they opened their feet and dropped little wrapped parcels on Elsa. The girl screamed when mud and animal dung splattered all over her. Immediately, everyone remaining beside the pyre was busy trying to clean her up. Laurent noticed with satisfaction that the line of soldiers who had guarded the rear of the cemetery had already dissolved so the approach of Albert and his army happened more or less unnoticed. He sent Jerome to the central fountain. His brother filled his feathers with as much water as he could and unloaded it on the soldiers near the tomb. Laurent sent Rene and Jorge to do the same, happy to notice a small hand slip through the tomb's grill to snatch up another shirt.

Seeing that his brothers and Jorge kept Pierre and his soldiers busy and Elsa distracted, Laurent flew to the cemetery's rear gate and opened it which proved rather difficult without hands. When the gate finally swung open, a wave of tiny animals shot through. Moles, mice, birds–even insects–were speeding toward the tomb. He flew ahead of them and dropped a feather now and then to mark the way. He wasn't really happy with just small animals, but they might just be enough to divert Pierre and Elsa long enough so he could free Michelle.

When he reached the tomb, he found that two soldiers were dragging Michelle toward the pyre. Either Pierre had decided his brothers were close enough to the ground or, more likely, Elsa had had enough and used her mind control on them. Instinctively Laurent landed and slipped into the gap between the tomb and the machine. It swished and another shirt came out. Then the gadget fell silent. Laurent looked at the shirt, then at his half-conscious sister, then at the shirt again. *So little time.*

Jorge flew directly into the torch that one of the soldiers had fetched while two others had tied Michelle to the pole in the middle of the pyre. Due to her injured arm, they bound her with a rope around her chest, leaving her standing with one arm hugging the other.

Two more soldiers came with torches, and more wet swans doused them. Then the wave of small animals hit and pandemonium broke out. Elsa tried frantically to climb something, anything, even if it was a soldier, just to get out of the way of the mice, and soldiers ran around cursing and trying to shake off moles, mice, and birds. Laurent grabbed the shirt with his beak and waddled toward Michelle. It wasn't easy to evade the stomping soldiers, but he managed fine until Albert's real army arrived.

Bears, wolves, foxes, deer, and more attacked what was left of Pierre's men. Jorge, Jerome, and Rene had knocked Elsa over and were hitting her with their wings as hard as they could, while Didier and Francois were trying to pull the wood off the pyre. A bunch of mice were climbing the pole to chew on the rope holding Michelle. Above them, a swan honked. Laurent looked up and saw Albert fly toward him. *Wow*, he thought. *I never expected Albert to fly again.*

The landing was somewhat uncomfortable, mainly for the soldier Albert landed on, but his brother came down without crashing. He looked around and squealed with delight.

"I did it! They're all here." He hopped from one foot to the other.

"Slip into the shirt," Laurent called and spread the loose fabric on the ground as best he could. For once, Albert did as he was told without hesitation. Laurent honked as loudly as he could, flapping his wings until he saw Michelle look his way. Her smile brightened the day. With her unhurt hand, she began to untie the shirts around her belly. Each time she held one up, Laurent called out a name.

"Jorge!" The swan swept in and slipped into the shirt. He looked ridiculous in it.

Next, Laurent donned a shirt himself. It tingled on his skin despite his feathers.

"Rene!"

"Jerome!"

Laurent noticed an eerie glow around the shirt-wearing swans. Elsa screamed at the top of her lungs at the soldiers to cut the shirts, but the men were way too busy fighting the animals.

"Didier, Francois! You'll have to put your shirts on at the same time."

"No problem, brother." The twins swooped in, pecking Elsa on the way, landed in front of Michelle, and wound their heads into the two final shirts. The glow around the swans intensified, and Laurent grew hot.

"You can go home now," Albert called to his friends.

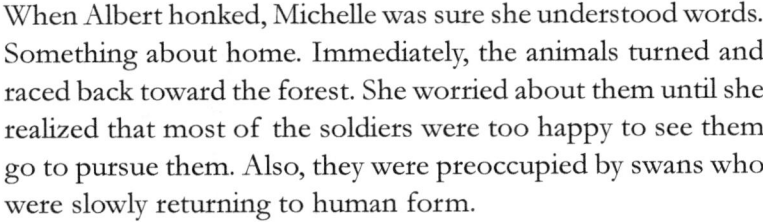

When Albert honked, Michelle was sure she understood words. Something about home. Immediately, the animals turned and raced back toward the forest. She worried about them until she realized that most of the soldiers were too happy to see them go to pursue them. Also, they were preoccupied by swans who were slowly returning to human form.

"We did it!" Michelle tugged at the rope around her chest and it ripped. Just in case the mice that had gnawed through it were still there, she thanked them. Before she could step off the pyre, something soft touched her chest. Warmth spread through her body and the pain in her arm subsided. *The ghost! How come it can be here during the day?* She shaded her eyes and gazed down her front. A tiny ball of light sat between her breasts. It flickered on and off in a strange pattern. Michelle had the feeling that it wanted something from her but didn't understand.

"You'll pay for that!" Elsa walked toward her, hands raised, spitting out strange words that sliced through the morning air and made the hairs on Michelle's arms stand up. Elsa's fingers played with two green balls of fire that grew with every word she spoke. Michelle stepped backward hurriedly and ducked when Elsa threw the first ball. The tree behind her exploded in a shower of green sparks.

Michelle looked down at the spark on her chest. It blinked rapidly as if trying to explain something. "I don't understand, but whatever you have in mind, do it."

Energy flowed through her body, and a low voice in her brain whispered, "Thank you."

Then her world turned into white-hot anger.

When Laurent regained his human body, Pierre stood over him with a gun in his hand. Before he could pull the trigger, though, Jorge slammed something against his temple and Pierre crumpled to the ground.

"Michelle!" Jorge called, and ran off. Extremely glad to be back in human form, Laurent struggled to his feet. *The only thing I'll miss is flying without the aid of airships*, he thought, and looked for his sister.

Elsa hurled a green ball of fire against Jorge. At the last second he threw himself to the ground. The fire only singed his hair.

Laurent ripped the rapier from Pierre's belt and attacked without a sound. Elsa called up another fireball, but had to throw it at him before it was big enough to cause much damage. The rapier deflected it easily and then cut into Elsa's shoulder. She screamed in pain and staggered back toward the tomb.

Before Laurent could follow, Michelle made a beeline for Elsa with her arms stretched out. As she passed him, Laurent noticed something as fragile as a cobweb between her arms.

Elsa lifted her arms as if to avert whatever was coming. The barely visible net caught her, moved through her, and pushed out a dark, smoky cloud. The body stayed behind as if suspended in time.

Laurent froze. His heart contracted but his legs refused to move. Something bright spilled from Michelle's body, pushing around the smoky cloud while simultaneously slipping into Elsa's body. The cloud struggled against the barely visible fibers without much success. Laurent brandished his rapier and stepped up beside his sister. Michelle shook her head like she was in a dream.

The second the light vanished fully into Elsa's body, it had to let go of the net. Instantly the dark cloud attacked Laurent and Michelle. Laurent pierced it with his rapier, and it retreated.

Michelle danced around it and ripped the cover off her machine. Keeping the cloud dodging his rapier, Laurent watched with interest how she attached the threads of the net to her machine. Then she knelt and turned the crank. The machine came to life once again.

The cloud howled as it was ripped backwards, but the mechanism relentlessly sucked it in.

"Get what you deserve." Michelle stood beside her brother. Then she rubbed her arm, and Laurent remembered how the guard had smashed the bones.

"Shall I fetch the physician?"

"No. Elsa healed the bones. The muscles just hurt a bit but that'll heal soon." Michelle went to Elsa, who'd crumpled to the ground, and helped her up. "Everything alright?"

Elsa stood in front of them with vacant eyes. Light danced over her, barely visible in the sun.

"Come on, you said you could get back in once the witch was out of your body." Michelle bent forward, as if listening to something.

Suddenly all the pieces of the puzzle fell in place for Laurent. His ghost must have been the real Elsa, and her body had been occupied by the witch. He looked at the machine that was still jabbering away, knitting witch and net into a loose fabric. It was nearly done. The dark, cloudy stuff of the witch's being swirled angrily between the net's loops. There wasn't enough for a whole shirt but that didn't matter one bit. Gently, Laurent pried the fabric off the knitter and carried it to the pyre where he laid it on the wood.

"Does anyone have some fire?" he called to the people standing around looking confused. One soldier came forward with matches, and Laurent started the fire. It took a while to eat through the whole pyre, and he could see how the black smoke fought its prison to escape, but the knitter had done a good job. Soon it was swallowed by the fire.

At that moment, Michelle jubilated and Pierre sat up.

"What happened?" he asked, looking around in confusion. "What am I doing on a cemetery?"

"She did it!" Michelle grabbed Laurent's arm and pulled him around to face Elsa. The princess looked at him, wide-eyed.

"You killed her."

"I promised I would."

"How can I ever thank you for that?"

Laurent looked around at the bewildered Pierre, at his brothers in their human form with Albert hiding a mouse in his pocket, at Jorge who stood with his arm around Michelle's shoulder, and back at Elsa. Her eyes sparkled like twin stars. Instead of an answer, he stepped forward, pulled her into his arms and pressed his lips against hers. Together they melted into a kiss that would unite two kingdoms.

HOME AND HEARTH
based on The Three Little Piglets by Joseph Jacobs

"What are we going to do now?" Stomper, the eldest piglet, asked. "The wolf is still standing in front of your house, little brother."

Smart, the youngest piglet, peeked through the gap in the window shutters. It was true. The wolf stood right in front of the entrance door, rubbing the burnt patch at the top end of his tail. There was nothing much they could do at the moment. Smart decided to play for time. "Let's prepare a soup for lunch," he said to his bigger brothers. "After all, we already have the fire going."

When they sat down to eat, the wolf banged at the door. "Piglet Smart. Give me one of your brothers. Just one!" He banged some more when the piglets remained silent. "My kids are starving, and so am I. You won't need both of your brothers."

The piglets Stomper and Plump clung to their younger brother's arms.

"Don't let him in," they whispered.

"They are my brothers for better or worse," Smart cried at the closed door.

"Then, I will sit in front of your house until you realize just how it is to be hungry. And then, I'll take the first piglet that comes out to buy food." A thud sounded from the massive wooden door, and when Smart peeked through the gap in the window shutters again, he could just about make out the wolf's gray, pointed ears close to their door.

"Oh no," Plump said. "What if we run out of food?"

Smart looked at the pile of fruit and vegetables their mother had given them and which they had put in his kitchen. They wouldn't starve any time soon. He glared at Stomper who was stuffing his face.

"What?" Stomper spoke with his mouth full. "I'm just making sure I get enough."

Smart sighed and turned back to the door. "Wolf?"

"Giving up already?"

"We could share our potatoes with you. Or our carrots. If you're fast there will even be some salad left." Smart didn't really want to share their provisions, but if it meant getting rid of the predator, he'd fight his brothers for every scrap of food there was.

"I'm a meat eater, dummy. I can't eat vegetables. I tried and got severe stomach aches." The wolf growled, and Stomper hid under the kitchen table, the only piece of furniture in the house. Plump dropped on his back pretending to be dead. Smart thought that both of them were not just silly but outright useless. There had to be something he could do. Maybe he could find a solution if he went into town. But the wolf would never let him go, would he? Well, it was worth a try. Maybe there was a hunter in town who needed a wolf-pelt. Smart stood straighter and spoke to the wolf behind the door.

"I want to make a bargain." He looked back at his brothers who were fighting over the food, eating everything although they couldn't possibly be hungry any more. "My brothers are

70

behaving like pigs, and I don't fancy starving. What if I can find a job that will feed us as well as it would feed you?"

"You won't find a job. Don't you think I tried?" Suddenly, the wolf didn't sound so much like a starving predator any more. His voice sounded hollow and full of resignation.

"Would you let me out, so I can try?" Smart held his breath. Was it wise to trust a hungry wolf?

The wolf remained silent for a very long time. Then he sighed. "Fine. But if you come back without work for both of us, I'll eat you."

With his heart thumping like a steam engine piston, Smart unlocked the door and left the house. When the wolf made no move to attack him, he locked the door again. His throat felt as if he hadn't drunken a drop of water in three days when he addressed the wolf. "I will ask around in town. Is there anything you're good at?"

"Aside from blowing and stomping down houses?" The wolf laughed mirthlessly. "I can eat a lot. I'm a great hunter, and I can be silent as a ghost."

There was a glint in his eyes that made Smart wish to be someplace else. So he didn't linger but hurried toward the town.

An hour later, he reached the outskirts of the town with sore feet. Who could have known that it was so far away from the village where he had built his house? Wearily he looked around for either a job that'd suit the wolf or a hunter who could rid him and his brothers of the wolf. He talked to countless people, but the day went by and he had nothing to show for his efforts but an apple that a caring soul had given him. Tired and unhappy, Smart sat on the steps of a big house in a row of big houses. The wide gate beside the normal entrance door suggested that it belonged to a farmer, although how a farmer could farm anything inside a town evaded Smart. He bit in his apple when an angry voice called out.

"I'm not paying you for telling me that it won't work. You promised you could do this!"

"I only promised I'd have a look," a second voice said, equally loud but less angry. "The other houses are too close. It's impossible to take down your barn without damaging them."

Two men approached the gate. The owner of the house was red in the face and fought to keep his hands from balling up into fists. The second man said a hurried farewell and left.

"Pah! Incompetent fool." The farmer spit on the ground. Then he noticed Smart. "What are you staring at?"

Smart's thoughts raced. Was this the chance he'd been looking for? "Sorry, sir. I couldn't help overhearing. You need a barn to be taken down?" He held his breath. After all, that was what the wolf had claimed to be good at.

"I need it replaced, but all the builders I asked so far claim it's impossible to take apart." The farmer looked him up and down. "Are you trying to tell me you can do a thing the finest builders in town can't?"

"Well, I've got a destruction specialist at hand, and I'm a good builder myself." Smart stood as straight as he could to look competent. He knew it wasn't easy for humans to trust in a piglets abilities, he'd lived through the rejection the whole day, but he hoped the farmer would be desperate enough.

The farmer scratched his head. "I've got nothing to lose, right? Be here first thing in the morning."

"Yes sir." Smart bowed. Encouraged by the gruff acceptance, he dared to make a request. "Sir, my specialist is starving, and I fear for my life if I return to him empty handed. Do you think you could spare a tiny morsel of meat?"

The farmer glared at him. "Next you'll want a bag of gold up front."

"No, sir, just a little bit of meat so I can fetch my partner safely." Smart tried not to fidget.

The farmer turned and left wordlessly, and Smart didn't know what to do. A few minutes later, the man returned with a small piece of ham.

"It's from a non-talking pig," he said.

Smart was surprised that the farmer blushed. He knew humans ate pigs. That was the reason why he and his brothers had decided to start looking for their fortune in the first place. He took the ham with gratitude. It looked dried out, but Smart was sure the wolf wouldn't mind. He waited until the farmer had closed the gate, swallowed the rest of his apple, and hurried back home.

It was already dark when he neared his house, but the wolf was still standing in front of the door. He eyed Smart, and a dribble of saliva hung from his flew. "Well, have you got a job?"

"I might." The hairs in Smart's neck stood up. The hungry expression on the wolf's face was even more pronounced than in the morning. "We're supposed to be in town first thing in the morning, and for a farmer the morning starts at dawn. Here's a little refreshment for the way." He held out the ham. The wolf grabbed it, scratching Smart's wrist in his greed, and began chewing on the leathery meat. Smart was extremely glad that it wasn't his own backside his partner-to-be was eating.

"I'll see you in the morning, I guess." The wolf stepped aside and allowed Smart to enter his house.

Stomper and Plump were lying on their back amidst the leftover vegetables and snored. Smart curled up under the table in a relatively clean spot and slept too.

Long before dawn, the wolf hammered at the door and called, "Time to go!"

Smart was so tired, he barely managed to eat a little. Silently, he and his new *partner* walked the long distance to the town. The wolf's starved expression had eased a little but not much, which woke Smart more thoroughly than the cold water he had used. As they neared the farmer's house, Smart explained about the barn. The farmer was already waiting for them, eager to show them the premises.

"I offered the other builders fourteen pieces of gold and three silver," he said and pointed to a small timber-frame barn standing in a ring of neighboring houses. "It's too small."

Wordlessly, the wolf walked around the construction, bumping his fist against the wattle and daub walls here and there, while Smart determined how much room there'd be for a new barn.

"If my partner can remove the old barn, I can build you a new one twice as big." He looked to the wolf who had finished his tour. "Do you think it's possible?"

"Fifteen pieces of gold and eight silver, building materials extra," the wolf said. "Plus another ham up front. All in a written contract so you can't back out when the barn is down."

The farmer's eyes widened. "You really can take it down without danger to my neighbors?"

The wolf nodded, which surprised the farmer so much that he hurried to fetch the ham the wolf had requested and a scribe for the contract. When it was signed, the wolf stepped closer to the barn and sucked in air.

"We'd better look for cover," Smart suggested. "There'll be a lot of debris flying though the air."

The farmer took him and the scribe into the living room of his house where they could watch through the big glass window.

The wolf walked around the barn. And he huffed, and he puffed, and he blew the barn in, one side at a time. A big cloud of dust billowed up whenever another wall fell. Soon, the wolf was invisible, but when the dust settled, the barn was lying on the ground in pieces and the wolf stood there, chewing his slightly gritty ham.

Smart hurried out to him and congratulated him on a job well done. "Now I'll only need to get my brothers so we can clear up this mess and start building."

The farmer took the wolf's hand, shook it, and handed him a purse. "I am so thrilled. You earned your money well. Wait until my friend sees this. He'll want to hire you on the spot."

Smart and the wolf extracted themselves from the grateful farmer with great difficulties.

"You know, I think I'll buy a pony and a cart from my share," Smart said on the way back to his house. "All this walking is a little too much for my short legs."

The wolf laughed. "Do you really think there'll be more people in town who need houses blown down?"

"The scribe knew of seventeen alone. I think we'll be in business for quite a while." Smart smiled up at the wolf, and suddenly the toothy grin didn't seem half as scary as it was before.

"To Wolf and Pig," the wolf said and bit off a piece of ham.

Smart thought of his brothers. It was time they started to work for their upkeep. After all, a lot of help was needed to clear away debris and carry building materials.

"I think we should call ourselves Wolf, Smart, and Co.," he said and smiled at his partner.

THE ORIGINAL: THE WILD SWANS

Hans Christian Andersen

There are countless variations of this fairy tale from many countries (The Seven Ravens, Eleven Swans, The Six Swans, The Girl and her Brothers). I used only those motives in my retelling that carry importance for me.

Far away in the land to which the swallows fly when it is winter, dwelt a king who had eleven sons, and one daughter, named Eliza. The eleven brothers were princes, and each went to school with a star on his breast, and a sword by his side. They wrote with diamond pencils on gold slates, and learnt their lessons so quickly and read so easily that every one might know they were princes. Their sister Eliza sat on a little stool of plate-glass, and had a book full of pictures, which had cost as much as half a kingdom. Oh, these children were indeed happy, but it was not to remain so always. Their father, who was king of the country, married a very wicked queen, who did not love the poor children at all. They knew this from the very first day after the wedding. In the palace there were great festivities, and the children played at receiving company; but instead of having, as usual, all the cakes and apples that were left, she gave them some sand in a tea-cup, and told them to pretend it was cake. The week after, she sent little Eliza into the country to a peasant and his wife, and then she told the king so many untrue things about the young princes, that he gave himself no more trouble respecting them.

"Go out into the world and get your own living," said the queen. "Fly like great birds, who have no voice." But she could not make them ugly as she wished, for they were turned into eleven beautiful wild swans. Then, with a strange cry, they flew through the windows of the palace, over the park, to the forest beyond. It was early morning when they passed the peasant's cottage, where their sister Eliza lay asleep in her room. They hovered over the roof, twisted their long necks and flapped their wings, but no one heard them or saw them, so they were at last obliged to fly away, high up in the clouds; and over the wide world they flew till they came to a thick, dark wood, which stretched far away to the seashore. Poor little Eliza was alone in her room playing with a green leaf, for she had no other playthings, and she pierced a hole through the leaf, and looked through it at the sun, and it was as if she saw her brothers' clear eyes, and when the warm sun shone on her cheeks, she thought of all the kisses they had given her. One day passed just like another; sometimes the winds rustled through the leaves of the rose-bush, and would whisper to the roses, "Who can be more beautiful than you!" But the roses would shake their heads, and say, "Eliza is." And when the old woman sat at the cottage door on Sunday, and read her hymn-book, the wind would flutter the leaves, and say to the book, "Who can be more pious than you?" and then the hymn-book would answer "Eliza." And the roses and the hymn-book told the real truth. At fifteen she returned home, but when the queen saw how beautiful she was, she became full of spite and hatred towards her. Willingly would she have turned her into a swan, like her brothers, but she did not dare to do so yet, because the king wished to see his daughter. Early one morning the queen went into the bath-room; it was built of marble, and had soft cushions, trimmed with the most beautiful tapestry. She took three toads with her, and kissed them, and said to one, "When Eliza comes to the bath, seat yourself upon her head, that she may become as stupid as you are." Then she said to another, "Place yourself on her forehead, that she may become as ugly as you are, and that her father may not know her." "Rest on her heart," she whispered to the third, "then she will have evil inclinations, and suffer in consequence." So she put the toads into the clear water, and they turned green immediately. She next called Eliza, and helped her to undress and get into the bath. As Eliza dipped her head under the water, one of the toads sat on her hair, a second on her forehead, and a third on her breast, but she did not seem to notice them, and when she rose out of the water, there were three red poppies floating upon it. Had not the creatures been venomous or been kissed by the witch, they would have been changed into red roses. At all events they became flowers, because they had rested on Eliza's head, and on her heart. She was too good and too innocent for witchcraft to have any power over her. When the wicked queen saw this, she rubbed her face with walnut-juice, so that she was quite brown; then she tangled her beautiful hair and smeared it with disgusting ointment, till it was quite impossible to recognize the beautiful Eliza.

When her father saw her, he was much shocked, and declared she was not his daughter. No one but the watch-dog and the swallows knew her; and they were only poor animals, and could say nothing. Then poor Eliza wept, and thought of her eleven brothers, who were all away. Sorrowfully, she stole away from the palace, and walked, the whole day, over fields and moors, till she came to the great forest. She knew not in what direction to go; but she was so unhappy, and longed so for her brothers, who had been, like herself, driven out into the world, that she was determined to seek them. She had been but a short time in the wood when night came on, and she quite lost the path; so she laid herself down on the soft moss, offered up her evening prayer, and leaned her head against the stump of a tree. All nature was still, and the soft, mild air fanned her forehead. The light of hundreds of glow-worms shone amidst the grass and the moss, like green fire; and if she touched a twig with her hand, ever so lightly, the brilliant insects fell down around her, like shooting-stars.

All night long she dreamt of her brothers. She and they were children again, playing together. She saw them writing with their diamond pencils on golden slates, while she looked at the beautiful picture-book which had cost half a kingdom. They were not writing lines and letters, as they used to do; but descriptions of the noble deeds they had performed, and of all they had discovered and seen. In the picture-book, too, everything was living. The birds sang, and the people came out of the book, and spoke to Eliza and her brothers; but, as the leaves turned over, they darted back again to their places, that all might be in order.

When she awoke, the sun was high in the heavens; yet she could not see him, for the lofty trees spread their branches thickly over her head; but his beams were glancing through the leaves here and there, like a golden mist. There was a sweet fragrance from the fresh green verdure, and the birds almost perched upon her shoulders. She heard water rippling from a number of springs, all flowing in a lake with golden sands. Bushes grew thickly round the lake, and at one spot an opening had been made by a deer, through which Eliza went down to the water. The lake was so clear that, had not the wind rustled the branches of the trees and the bushes, so that they moved, they would have appeared as if painted in the depths of the lake; for every leaf was reflected in the water, whether it stood in the shade or the sunshine. As soon as Eliza saw her own face, she was quite terrified at finding it so brown and ugly; but when she wetted her little hand, and rubbed her eyes and forehead, the white skin gleamed forth once more; and, after she had undressed, and dipped herself in the fresh water, a more beautiful king's daughter could not be found in the wide world. As soon as she had dressed herself again, and braided her long hair, she went to the bubbling spring, and drank some water out of the hollow of her hand. Then she wandered far into the forest, not knowing whither she went. She thought of her brothers, and felt sure that God would not forsake her. It is God who makes the wild apples grow in the wood, to satisfy the hungry, and He now led her to one of these trees, which was so loaded with fruit, that the boughs bent beneath the weight. Here she held her noonday repast, placed props under the boughs, and then went into the gloomiest depths of the forest. It was so still that she could hear the sound of her own footsteps, as well as the rustling of every withered leaf which she crushed under her feet. Not a bird was to be seen, not a sunbeam could penetrate through the large, dark boughs of the trees. Their lofty trunks stood so close together, that, when she looked before her, it seemed as if she were enclosed within trellis-work. Such solitude she had never known before. The night was very dark. Not a single glow-worm glittered in the moss.

Sorrowfully she laid herself down to sleep; and, after a while, it seemed to her as if the branches of the trees parted over her head, and that the mild eyes of angels looked down upon her from heaven. When she awoke in the morning, she knew not whether she had dreamt this, or if it had really been so. Then she continued her wandering; but she had not gone many steps forward, when she met an old woman with berries in her basket, and she gave her a few to eat. Then Eliza asked her if she had not seen eleven princes riding through the forest.

"No," replied the old woman, "But I saw yesterday eleven swans, with gold crowns on their heads, swimming on the river close by." Then she led Eliza a little distance farther to a sloping bank, and at the foot of it wound a little river. The trees on its banks stretched their long leafy branches across the water towards each other, and where the growth prevented them from meeting naturally, the roots had torn themselves away from the ground, so that the branches might mingle their foliage as they hung over the water. Eliza bade the old woman farewell, and walked by the flowing river, till she reached the shore of the open sea. And there, before the young maiden's eyes, lay the glorious ocean, but not a sail appeared on its surface, not even a boat could be seen. How was she to go farther? She noticed how the countless pebbles on the sea-shore had been smoothed and rounded by the action of the water. Glass, iron, stones, everything that lay there mingled together, had taken its shape from the same power, and felt as smooth, or even smoother than her own delicate hand. "The water rolls on without weariness," she said, "till all that is hard becomes smooth; so will I be unwearied in my task. Thanks for your lessons, bright rolling waves; my heart tells me you will lead me to my dear brothers." On the foam-covered sea-weeds, lay eleven white swan feathers, which she gathered up and placed together. Drops of water lay upon them; whether they were dew-drops or tears no one could say. Lonely as it was on the sea-shore, she did not observe it, for the ever-moving sea showed more changes in a few hours than the most varying lake could produce during a whole year. If a black heavy cloud arose, it was as if the sea said, "I can look dark and angry too;" and then the wind blew, and the waves turned to white foam as they rolled. When the wind slept, and the clouds glowed with the red sunlight, then the sea looked like a rose leaf. But however quietly its white glassy surface rested, there was still a motion on the shore, as its waves rose and fell like the breast of a sleeping child. When the sun was about to set, Eliza saw eleven white swans with golden crowns on their heads, flying towards the land, one behind the other, like a long white ribbon. Then Eliza went down the slope from the shore, and hid herself behind the bushes. The swans alighted quite close to her and flapped their great white wings. As soon as the sun had disappeared under the water, the feathers of the swans fell off, and eleven beautiful princes, Eliza's brothers, stood near her. She uttered a loud cry, for, although they were very much changed, she knew them immediately. She sprang into their arms, and called them each by name. Then, how happy the princes were at meeting their little sister again, for they recognized her, although she had grown so tall and beautiful. They laughed, and they wept, and very soon understood how wickedly their mother had acted to them all. "We brothers," said the eldest, "fly about as wild swans, so long as the sun is in the sky; but as soon as it sinks behind the hills, we recover our human shape. Therefore must we always be near a resting place for our feet before sunset; for if we should be flying towards the clouds at the time we recovered our natural shape as men, we should sink deep into the sea. We do not dwell here, but in a land just as fair, that lies beyond the ocean, which we have to cross for a long distance; there is no island in our passage upon which we could pass, the night; nothing but a little rock rising out of the sea, upon which we can scarcely stand with safety, even closely crowded together. If the sea is rough, the foam dashes over us, yet we thank God even for this rock; we have passed whole nights upon it, or we should never have reached our beloved fatherland, for our flight across the sea occupies two of the longest days in the year. We have permission to visit out home once in every year, and to remain eleven days, during which we fly across the forest to look once more at the palace where our father dwells, and where we were born, and at the church, where our mother lies buried. Here it seems as if the very trees and bushes were related to us. The wild horses leap over the plains as we have seen them in our childhood. The charcoal burners sing the old songs, to which we have danced as children. This is our fatherland, to which we are drawn by loving ties; and here we have found you, our dear little sister., Two days longer we can remain here, and then must we fly away to a beautiful land which is not our home; and how can we take you with us? We have neither ship nor boat."

"How can I break this spell?" said their sister. And then she talked about it nearly the whole night, only slumbering for a few hours. Eliza was awakened by the rustling of the swans' wings as they soared above. Her brothers were again changed to swans, and they flew in circles wider and wider, till they were far away; but one of them, the youngest swan, remained behind, and laid his head in his sister's lap, while she stroked his wings; and they remained together the whole day. Towards evening, the rest came back, and as the sun went down they resumed their natural forms. "To-morrow," said one, "we shall fly away, not to return again till a whole year has passed. But we cannot leave you here. Have you courage to go with us? My arm is strong enough to carry you through the wood; and will not all our wings be strong enough to fly with you over the sea?"

"Yes, take me with you," said Eliza. Then they spent the whole night in weaving a net with the pliant willow and rushes. It was very large and strong. Eliza laid herself down on the net, and when the sun rose, and her brothers again became wild swans, they took up the net with their beaks, and flew up to the clouds with their dear sister, who still slept. The sunbeams fell on her face, therefore one of the swans soared over her head, so that his broad wings might shade her. They were far from the land when Eliza woke. She thought she must still be dreaming, it seemed so strange to her to feel herself being carried so high in the air over the sea. By her side lay a branch full of beautiful ripe berries, and a bundle of sweet roots; the youngest of her brothers had gathered them for her, and placed them by her side. She smiled her thanks to him; she knew it was the same who had hovered over her to shade her with his wings. They were now so high, that a large ship beneath them looked like a white sea-gull skimming the waves. A great cloud floating behind them appeared like a vast mountain, and upon it Eliza saw her own shadow and those of the eleven swans, looking gigantic in size. Altogether it formed a more beautiful picture than she had ever seen; but as the sun rose higher, and the clouds were left behind, the shadowy picture vanished away. Onward the whole day they flew through the air like a winged arrow, yet more slowly than usual, for they had their sister to carry. The weather seemed inclined to be stormy, and Eliza watched the sinking sun with great anxiety, for the little rock in the ocean was not yet in sight. It appeared to her as if the swans were making great efforts with their wings. Alas! she was the cause of their not advancing more quickly. When the sun set, they would change to men, fall into the sea and be drowned. Then she offered a prayer from her inmost heart, but still no appearance of the rock. Dark clouds came nearer, the gusts of wind told of a coming storm, while from a thick, heavy mass of clouds the lightning burst forth flash after flash. The sun had reached the edge of the sea, when the swans darted down so swiftly, that Eliza's head trembled; she believed they were falling, but they again soared onward. Presently she caught sight of the rock just below them, and by this time the sun was half hidden by the waves. The rock did not appear larger than a seal's head thrust out of the water. They sunk so rapidly, that at the moment their feet touched the rock, it shone only like a star, and at last disappeared like the last spark in a piece of burnt paper. Then she saw her brothers standing closely round her with their arms linked together. There was but just room enough for them, and not the smallest space to spare. The sea dashed against the rock, and covered them with spray. The heavens were lighted up with continual flashes, and peal after peal of thunder rolled. But the sister and brothers sat holding each other's hands, and singing hymns, from which they gained hope and courage. In the early dawn the air became calm and still, and at sunrise the swans flew away from the rock with Eliza. The sea was still rough, and from their high position in the air, the white foam on the dark green waves looked like millions of swans swimming on the water. As the sun rose higher, Eliza saw before her, floating on the air, a range of mountains, with shining masses of ice on their summits. In the centre, rose a castle apparently a mile long, with rows of columns, rising one above another, while, around it, palm-trees waved and flowers bloomed as large as mill wheels. She asked if this was the land to which they were hastening. The swans shook their heads, for what she beheld were the beautiful ever-changing cloud palaces of the "Fata Morgana," into which no mortal can enter. Eliza was still gazing at the scene, when mountains, forests, and castles melted away, and twenty stately churches rose in their stead, with high towers and pointed gothic windows. Eliza even fancied she could hear the tones of the organ, but it was the music of the murmuring sea which she heard. As they drew nearer to the churches, they also changed into a fleet of ships, which seemed to be sailing beneath her; but as she looked again, she found it was only a sea mist gliding over the ocean. So there continued to pass before her eyes a constant change of scene, till at last she saw the real land to which they were bound, with its blue mountains, its cedar forests, and its cities and palaces. Long before the sun went down, she sat on a rock, in front of a large cave, on the floor of which the over-grown yet delicate green creeping plants looked like an embroidered carpet. "Now we shall expect to hear what you dream of to-night," said the youngest brother, as he showed his sister her bedroom.

"Heaven grant that I may dream how to save you," she replied. And this thought took such hold upon her mind that she prayed earnestly to God for help, and even in her sleep she continued to pray. Then it appeared to her as if she were flying high in the air, towards the cloudy palace of the "Fata Morgana," and a fairy came out to meet her, radiant and beautiful in appearance, and yet very much like the old woman who had given her berries in the wood, and who had told her of the swans with golden crowns on their heads. "Your brothers can be released," said she, "if you have only courage and perseverance. True, water is softer than your own delicate hands, and yet it polishes stones into shapes; it feels no pain as your fingers would feel, it has no soul, and cannot suffer such agony and torment as you will have to endure. Do you see the stinging nettle which I hold in my hand? Quantities of the same sort grow round the cave in which you sleep, but none will be of any use to you unless they grow upon the graves in a churchyard. These you must gather even while they burn blisters on your hands. Break them to pieces with your hands and feet, and they will become flax, from which you must spin and weave eleven coats with long sleeves; if these are then thrown over the eleven swans, the spell will be broken. But remember, that from the moment you commence your task until it is finished, even should it occupy years of your life, you must not speak. The first word you utter will pierce through the hearts of your brothers like a deadly dagger. Their lives hang upon your tongue. Remember all I have told you." And as she finished speaking, she touched her hand lightly with the nettle, and a pain, as of burning fire, awoke Eliza.

It was broad daylight, and close by where she had been sleeping lay a nettle like the one she had seen in her dream. She fell on her knees and offered her thanks to God. Then she went forth from the cave to begin her work with her delicate hands. She groped in amongst the ugly nettles, which burnt great blisters on her hands and arms, but she determined to bear it gladly if she could only release her dear brothers. So she bruised the nettles with her bare feet and spun the flax. At sunset her brothers returned and were very much frightened when they found her dumb. They believed it to be some new sorcery of their wicked step-mother. But when they saw her hands they understood what she was doing on their behalf, and the youngest brother wept, and where his tears fell the pain ceased, and the burning blisters vanished. She kept to her work all night, for she could not rest till she had released her dear brothers. During the whole of the following day, while her brothers were absent, she sat in solitude, but never before had the time flown so quickly. One coat was already finished and she had begun the second, when she heard the huntsman's horn, and was struck with fear. The sound came nearer and nearer, she heard the dogs barking, and fled with terror into the cave. She hastily bound together the nettles she had gathered into a bundle and sat upon them. Immediately a great dog came bounding towards her out of the ravine, and then another and another; they barked loudly, ran back, and then came again. In a very few minutes all the huntsmen stood before the cave, and the handsomest of them was the king of the country. He advanced towards her, for he had never seen a more beautiful maiden.

"How did you come here, my sweet child?" he asked. But Eliza shook her head. She dared not speak, at the cost of her brothers' lives. And she hid her hands under her apron, so that the king might not see how she must be suffering.

"Come with me," he said; "here you cannot remain. If you are as good as you are beautiful, I will dress you in silk and velvet, I will place a golden crown upon your head, and you shall dwell, and rule, and make your home in my richest castle." And then he lifted her on his horse. She wept and wrung her hands, but the king said, "I wish only for your happiness. A time will come when you will thank me for this." And then he galloped away over the mountains, holding her before him on this horse, and the hunters followed behind them. As the sun went down, they approached a fair royal city, with churches, and cupolas. On arriving at the castle the king led her into marble halls, where large fountains played, and where the walls and the ceilings were covered with rich paintings. But she had no eyes for all these glorious sights, she could only mourn and weep. Patiently she allowed the women to array her in royal robes, to weave pearls in her hair, and draw soft gloves over her blistered fingers. As she stood before them in all her rich dress, she looked so dazzingly beautiful that the court bowed low in her presence. Then the king declared his intention of making her his bride, but the archbishop shook his head, and whispered that the fair young maiden was only a witch who had blinded the king's eyes and bewitched his heart. But the king would not listen to this; he ordered the music to sound, the daintiest dishes to be served, and the loveliest maidens to dance. After-wards he led her through fragrant gardens and lofty halls, but not a smile appeared on her lips or sparkled in her eyes. She looked the very picture of grief. Then the king opened the door of a little chamber in which she. was to sleep; it was adorned with rich green tapestry, and resembled the cave in which he had found her. On the floor lay the bundle of flax which she had spun from the nettles, and under the ceiling hung the coat she had made. These things had been brought away from the cave as curiosities by one of the huntsmen.

"Here you can dream yourself back again in the old home in the cave," said the king; "here is the work with which you employed yourself. It will amuse you now in the midst of all this splendor to think of that time."

When Eliza saw all these things which lay so near her heart, a smile played around her mouth, and the crimson blood rushed to her cheeks. She thought of her brothers, and their release made her so joyful that she kissed the king's hand. Then he pressed her to his heart. Very soon the joyous church bells announced the marriage feast, and that the beautiful dumb girl out of the wood was to be made the queen of the country. Then the archbishop whispered wicked words in the king's ear, but they did not sink into his heart. The marriage was still to take place, and the archbishop himself had to place the crown on the bride's head; in his wicked spite, he pressed the narrow circlet so tightly on her forehead that it caused her pain. But a heavier weight encircled her heart—sorrow for her brothers. She felt not bodily pain. Her mouth was closed; a single word would cost the lives of her brothers. But she loved the kind, handsome king, who did everything to make her happy more and more each day; she loved him with all her heart, and her eyes beamed with the love she dared not speak. Oh! if she had only been able to confide in him and tell him of her grief. But dumb she must remain till her task was finished. Therefore at night she crept away into her little chamber, which had been decked out to look like the cave, and quickly wove one coat after another. But when she began the seventh she found she had no more flax. She knew that the nettles she wanted to use grew in the churchyard, and that she must pluck them herself. How should she get out there? "Oh, what is the pain in my fingers to the torment which my heart endures?" said she. "I must venture, I shall not be denied help from heaven." Then with a trembling heart, as if she were about to perform a wicked deed, she crept into the garden in the broad moonlight, and passed through the narrow walks and the deserted streets, till she reached the churchyard. Then she saw on one of the broad tombstones a group of ghouls. These hideous creatures took off their rags, as if they intended to bathe, and then clawing open the fresh graves with their long, skinny fingers, pulled out the dead bodies and ate the flesh! Eliza had to pass close by them, and they fixed their wicked glances upon her, but she prayed silently, gathered the burning nettles, and carried them home with her to the castle. One person only had seen her, and that was the archbishop—he was awake while everybody was asleep. Now he thought his opinion was evidently correct. All was not right with the queen. She was a witch, and had bewitched the king and all the people. Secretly he told the king what he had seen and what he feared, and as the hard words came from his tongue, the carved images of the saints shook their heads as if they would say. "It is not so. Eliza is innocent."

But the archbishop interpreted it in another way; he believed that they witnessed against her, and were shaking their heads at her wickedness. Two large tears rolled down the king's cheeks, and he went home with doubt in his heart, and at night he pretended to sleep, but there came no real sleep to his eyes, for he saw Eliza get up every night and disappear in her own chamber. From day to day his brow became darker, and Eliza saw it and did not understand the reason, but it alarmed her and made her heart tremble for her brothers. Her hot tears glittered like pearls on the regal velvet and diamonds, while all who saw her were wishing they could be queens. In the mean time she had almost finished her task; only one coat of mail was wanting, but she had no flax left, and not a single nettle. Once more only, and for the last time, must she venture to the churchyard and pluck a few handfuls. She thought with terror of the solitary walk, and of the horrible ghouls, but her will was firm, as well as her trust in Providence. Eliza went, and the king and the archbishop followed her. They saw her vanish through the wicket gate into the churchyard, and when they came nearer they saw the ghouls sitting on the tombstone, as Eliza had seen them, and the king turned away his head, for he thought she was with them—she whose head had rested on his breast that very evening. "The people must condemn her," said he, and she was very quickly condemned by every one to suffer death by fire. Away from the gorgeous regal halls was she led to a dark, dreary cell, where the wind whistled through the iron bars. Instead of the velvet and silk dresses, they gave her the coats of mail which she had woven to cover her, and the bundle of nettles for a pillow; but nothing they could give her would have pleased her more. She continued her task with joy, and prayed for help, while the street-boys sang jeering songs about her, and not a soul comforted her with a kind word. Towards evening, she heard at the grating the flutter of a swan's wing, it was her youngest brother—he had found his sister, and she sobbed for joy, although she knew that very likely this would be the last night she would have to live. But still she could hope, for her task was almost finished, and her brothers were come. Then the archbishop arrived, to be with her during her last hours, as he had promised the king. But she shook her head, and begged him, by looks and gestures, not to stay; for in this night she knew she must finish her task, otherwise all her pain and tears and sleepless nights would have been suffered in vain. The archbishop withdrew, uttering bitter words against her; but poor Eliza knew that she was innocent, and diligently continued her work.

The little mice ran about the floor, they dragged the nettles to her feet, to help as well as they could; and the thrush sat outside the grating of the window, and sang to her the whole night long, as sweetly as possible, to keep up her spirits.

It was still twilight, and at least an hour before sunrise, when the eleven brothers stood at the castle gate, and demanded to be brought before the king. They were told it could not be, it was yet almost night, and as the king slept they dared not disturb him. They threatened, they entreated. Then the guard appeared, and even the king himself, inquiring what all the noise meant. At this moment the sun rose. The eleven brothers were seen no more, but eleven wild swans flew away over the castle.

And now all the people came streaming forth from the gates of the city, to see the witch burnt. An old horse drew the cart on which she sat. They had dressed her in a garment of coarse sackcloth. Her lovely hair hung loose on her shoulders, her cheeks were deadly pale, her lips moved silently, while her fingers still worked at the green flax. Even on the way to death, she would not give up her task. The ten coats of mail lay at her feet, she was working hard at the eleventh, while the mob jeered her and said, "See the witch, how she mutters! She has no hymn-book in her hand. She sits there with her ugly sorcery. Let us tear it in a thousand pieces."

And then they pressed towards her, and would have destroyed the coats of mail, but at the same moment eleven wild swans flew over her, and alighted on the cart. Then they flapped their large wings, and the crowd drew on one side in alarm.

"It is a sign from heaven that she is innocent," whispered many of them; but they ventured not to say it aloud.

As the executioner seized her by the hand, to lift her out of the cart, she hastily threw the eleven coats of mail over the swans, and they immediately became eleven handsome princes; but the youngest had a swan's wing, instead of an arm; for she had not been able to finish the last sleeve of the coat.

"Now I may speak," she exclaimed. "I am innocent."

Then the people, who saw what happened, bowed to her, as before a saint; but she sank lifeless in her brothers' arms, overcome with suspense, anguish, and pain.

"Yes, she is innocent," said the eldest brother; and then he related all that had taken place; and while he spoke there rose in the air a fragrance as from millions of roses. Every piece of faggot in the pile had taken root, and threw out branches, and appeared a thick hedge, large and high, covered with roses; while above all bloomed a white and shining flower, that glittered like a star. This flower the king plucked, and placed in Eliza's bosom, when she awoke from her swoon, with peace and happiness in her heart. And all the church bells rang of themselves, and the birds came in great troops. And a marriage procession returned to the castle, such as no king had ever before seen.

THE DWARF AND THE TWINS

SNOW WHITE AND ROSE RED
Treasures Retold 1

Once upon a time in a world where magic and technology collide with unexpected consequences…

When Martin helps a pregnant woman to flee from the king's men, he doesn't know that the twins she bears will change his solitary life forever.

What if the Brother's Grimm misunderstood the dwarf in the original tale of "Snow White and Rose Red"?

The book includes a bonus story and the original fairy tale.

ISBN 978-3-95681-028-2
also available as eBook

Leave your eMail address so I can inform you about new releases, and this book will arrive as an eBook in your Inbox shortly after

http://www.katharinagerlach.com/readers

THE CHALLENGE
THE COLD HEART
Treasuers Retold 8

Once upon a time in a world where magic and technology collide with unexpected consequences…

Elfin, a male fairy, and Mikael, smith and inventor, want to know what's better, magic or technology. Unfortunately they didn't consider the human factor. Now they have to hurry to save their guinea pig and his loved-ones from the worst, before someone dies.

What if Wilhelm Hauff hadn't realized who was really responsible for „The Cold Heart"?

The book includes a bonus story and the original fairy tale.

ISBN 978-3-95681-073-2
also available as eBook